TWICE UPON A TIME

Sleeping Beauty

The One Who Took the Really Long Nap

WENDY MASS

SCHOLASTIC INC.
New York Toronto London Auckland
Sydney Mexico City New Delhi Hong Kong

For Stu, who I cannot write a book without
And for Mike, my real-life Prince Charming

ISBN 978-0-439-79658-3

12 11 10 9 8 7 6 5 4   12 13 14 15 16/0

Printed in the U.S.A.   40
First printing, September 2006

PROLOGUE

← The Prince →

When I finally reached her, all was completely still. The room was bathed in the kind of quiet where you couldn't hear a bee buzz or a toad croak even if you listened really, really hard. The dust motes hung motionless in the shafts of sunlight. The only sounds were my breath and my footfalls on the rug.

I gazed down at her, asleep on her bed of feather pillows. Never before had I seen beauty like this. Even if Mother had not long ago banned from the castle anything that might be considered pleasing to the eye, I would have never been prepared for this. Little did Mother know that tucked away on the grounds of our very own castle lay such loveliness.

The painting I had seen of the girl did not fully capture her true beauty. Her complexion was two part peaches and one part cream. Lips of cherry red. Raven-black hair, so silky it glowed. Her clothing was endearingly old-fashioned — layers of petticoats, a three-pointed collar, sleeves of lace. No one wore that anymore, but on her it looked fetching.

This was my moment. Here lay my destiny. I knew it as well as I knew my own name. (Okay, perhaps that last part was not exactly true because Mother had never given me a name. Nevertheless, I knew what I had to do.)

Before I got too nervous, I bent down and ever-so-gently let my lips fall upon hers. They felt as soft as they looked. While I had always assumed that the recipient of my first kiss would actually be awake and standing upright, it was pretty good as far as first kisses went.

I pulled away. At first, nothing happened. Then her eyelids began to flutter, and suddenly her eyes were wide open. I jumped back in surprise.

The girl sat bolt upright and stared at me. Her eyes were brighter than the bluest sky, although still a bit unfocused. She opened her mouth to speak, but only a squeak came out. She raised her hand to her neck in alarm, then cleared her throat a few times. She tried again. This time her voice was loud and clear.

"Pardon my rudeness," she said, "but WHO THE HECK ARE *YOU*?"

"Me?" I asked, surprised. No one had ever asked me that question before.

"Yes *you*," she said, looking wildly around the room. "Who are you?"

"Why, I'm . . . I'm the Prince," I replied, bowing gracefully.

"What are you doing here?" she asked breathlessly.

Her flushed cheeks were a deeper red now, and I was momentarily silenced by her beauty. I finally realized she was waiting for an answer.

"What am I doing here?" I said. "Why, I'm awakening you, Princess Rose."

Her nose crinkled in genuine confusion. "Awakening me? Awakening me from what?"

I stared at her. She honestly did not know what had happened to her! This required a delicate answer. I did not have much training in delicacy, but I tried my best. "You have been asleep for a hundred years. I do not know why. But you have lain in your castle all this time — hidden by vines and trees — protected with fairy magic from the outside world until I came to awaken you." Unsure what else to do, I bowed again, so deeply I almost tipped over.

The color drained from her face, then slowly refilled. Her eyes shook off a bit of their fogginess. She tried to get out of bed but stumbled. Her legs hadn't been used for a very long time. I quickly rushed to her aid. I held out my arm for support, and she took it. When she stood, the top of her head reached my nose. She examined my face for a moment.

"The past is slowly coming back to me," she finally said, letting go of my arm to smooth out her skirts. "Thank you for being the one to awaken me. Others have tried and failed."

I felt my eyebrows shoot up. "How can you know of the other attempts to enter your castle?"

She shook her head wearily. "It is a very long story. And I know nothing about you. I am not used to being alone in the company of a young man."

"Nor I a young woman," I replied. "Let us sit and get to know each other. I am quite sure we have a lot to talk about."

Before she could reply, something changed in the air around us. It seemed to thin out in some way. The room took on a dreamlike quality. A stab of fear hit me in the gut. Was I dreaming? Was the real me asleep outside the old castle where I'd spent so many frustrated nights? I saw her trying to reach for me, but it was too late — she was fading away.

All I could see was the space around her.

It was vast, and empty.

PART ONE

CHAPTER ONE

∽ Princess Rose, a hundred and sixteen years earlier ∽

On the day I was born, the heavens themselves opened up to shine rays of welcome down upon me. Or at least that's what Mama said. Mama wasn't born into royalty, like Papa, who was a prince before becoming a king, so she could get away with saying quaint things like that. She also said my nose was as cute and round as a ladybug's behind, and pretty much everyone knows ladybugs don't even *have* behinds.

When the midwife announced, "It's a girl!" whoops of joy and tears of happiness filled the air. Papa gave the whole kingdom the day off (except for the dung heap cleaners, but that is to be expected with an important job like that). I was placed in a bassinet overflowing with fine linen and feathers, and was swaddled in a blanket made from the efforts of the kingdom's finest silkworms. Life was good.

A few days after my birth, it was time for the ceremony where I would be officially named and have gifts bestowed upon me from the good fairies of the realm. Truly, it was only a formality, because I already had a name. My parents had dreamed of a child for many years, and they had long ago decided what to call me — if I were a girl, I would be named Gertrude (Gertie for short) after a favorite great-aunt of Mama's. But when I arrived, looking all rosy and perfect, they knew only one name would do me justice. I would be called Rose.

One by one the fairies arrived for my big day. The seven of them would be my godmothers and would protect me in times of trouble. Not that anyone expected any trouble, of course, which was fortunate because fairies were notoriously fickle, and often disappeared for decades at a time.

The ceremony began, and my name was officially added to the royal ledger, inscribed with ink made of pure silver. Papa had spared no expense for this event. While Mama fed me from a crystal baby bottle, the fairies were treated to a great feast of peacock and lamb and chocolate truffles. Their table was shorter than everyone else's since none of the fairies was taller than a yardstick. Their place settings were made of solid gold. The edges of the plates were encrusted with diamonds and rubies, while emeralds and sapphires ran down the stems of the silverware. These marvelous place settings were gifts for the fairies to take home with them, my parents' way of thanking them for the gifts they would bestow upon me at the end of the meal.

Much wine was consumed, and many toasts in my name were shouted to the roof beams. I lay in my bassinet, adorned for the occasion with a silver tiara and a pink taffeta dress. I smiled a toothless grin. One by one, the fairies formed a tight circle around me. It was time for the gift-giving.

The first fairy godmother said, "Princess Rose shall be the greatest beauty the world has ever known."

The second said, "She will be bright and clever."

The third said, "She shall be full of grace."

The fourth said, "She will be an excellent dancer."

The fifth said, "She will sing like a songbird."

The sixth said, "She shall play all kinds of music with equal perfection."

Mama and Papa nodded happily after each gift was announced. Mama, beloved throughout the kingdom for her goodness and charity to others, had suffered in silence without a child, and her dreams of having a perfect little daughter were finally coming true. But just as the final fairy leaned over me and opened her mouth, two of the castle guards came bursting into the room.

"Please, Your Highness," they said to Papa, bowing deeply, "forgive the intrusion. But an uninvited guest has barreled through the gate and is calling out your daughter's name. Here she comes now!"

My parents whirled around in alarm. A cold wind blew,

and along with it appeared an old fairy, white hair sticking out of her head in all directions. My parents stared at her, wide-eyed. Papa opened his mouth to speak, but closed it again when he saw the fury on the old woman's face.

"Why was I not invited to this christening?" she demanded. "As the eldest fairy in the realm, I am to be honored, not disgraced in this way."

"Please," Mama pleaded, wringing her hands. "We meant no disrespect. We thought you were . . . I mean . . . we had heard that you were —"

"Dead? You thought I was dead?"

Mama nodded miserably. She couldn't say the whole truth, which was that the fairy had gotten quite nasty in her old age — drank too much at parties, snapped at the staff, that sort of thing — so when word had reached the castle that she'd died, nobody had been too distressed about it.

The old fairy stood up straighter. This was not easy since she was bent practically in half. "As you can clearly see," she said mockingly, "the rumors of my death have been greatly exaggerated."

"Forgive us our oversight and join us for the celebration," Papa said, steering the old fairy toward the table. The other fairies hurried to sit back down. Papa snapped his fingers at the nearest page, who ran straight off to the pantry. He quickly returned with our finest china and set it before the fairy. She took one look at the place setting and slammed her hand down onto the table. Everyone grabbed their glasses so the wine wouldn't spill.

"I demand the same bejeweled gifts as the other fairies. How dare you further insult me in this way?"

Mama looked ready to faint. She did not like confrontation of any sort. "We . . . we only had these seven place settings commissioned. I promise you, we will order another and have it delivered to you at any place in the realm."

"I am tired of your excuses," the old fairy sneered. "It is time for me to deliver *my* gift now." She pushed back her chair, which screeched ominously on the stone floor.

Mother instinctively moved in front of my bassinet, but as the old fairy approached she had no choice but to step aside. I still gurgled happily, unaware that my life was about to change forever.

In a low voice, the fairy decreed, "The princess shall pierce her finger upon a spindle. At the first drop of blood, she shall die."

A gasp of shock and horror rose up in the room, and all was chaos. Chairs were tipped over, sobs soaked through silk napkins. Somehow the old fairy managed to slip away unseen.

"Wait! All is not lost!" A clear, sweet voice rose above the din of wails. Everyone stopped crying for a moment to find its source. The youngest of the fairies stepped forward and said, "I have not yet given my gift to the princess."

Mama's eyes filled with hope again. She clutched the fairy's arm. "Can you undo the curse?" she pleaded.

The young fairy shook her head and Mama crumpled dramatically into her chair.

"But I can weaken it," she said. The young fairy approached my bassinet, leaned over, and touched me gently on the forehead. "Young Rose, you shall indeed stick yourself with a spindle one day, but you shall not die of your wound. Instead, you shall fall into a deep sleep. This sleep will last at least one hundred years, until the right person awakens you."

Sighs of relief arose from every corner of the room. Papa waved over the royal scribe, who dipped his quill quickly into his portable inkwell and waited. Father cleared his throat and then boomed, "I proclaim here and now that all spindles and similar weaving or sewing equipment be removed from not only the castle but the surrounding towns and country-side as well. Anyone caught with a spindle in their home shall immediately be thrown into the castle dungeon."

"But, darling," Mama asked, her brow furrowed, "what will the townsfolk do if they cannot make or mend their own clothes?" Even with her daughter's safety on the line, Mama's kind heart could not be quieted.

"Do not worry, my dear," Papa said. "I shall be sure they are all provided for with clothing from another kingdom."

"But what of the tailors and seamstresses?" Mama asked. "How will they make a living?"

"We shall retrain them," Papa said, beginning to get exasperated.

Mama was satisfied, so Papa sent castle couriers to ride for miles around in every direction, making the announcement. Pages then went from house to house, collecting all the spindles and weaving wheels. Once the townsfolk were assured that my parents would not let them go without clothing, they happily turned everything over. Word of my beauty and wonderful disposition had already spread, so the townsfolk were eager to do their part to ensure my safety. And, truth be told, many a wife was only too happy not to have to spin anymore.

Life was good again.

CHAPTER TWO

← The Prince's Story, a hundred years after the birth of Princess Rose →

On the day of my birth, I was nearly eaten by an ogre. In this case, the ogre was my mother, the Queen. Everyone's family has a skeleton or two in the closet. In my family's case, those skeletons were both real (the unfortunate victims of my mother's ruthless appetite) and metaphorical, meaning that my family had a lot of secrets to hide from the general public.

The biggest secret, obviously, was that my mother possessed a healthy amount of ogre blood, passed down from a great-great-uncle who was a full ogre. She neglected to alert my father to her true nature until after he had fallen in love with her. This did not make her a bad person, exactly, just perhaps a bit sneaky. Mother looked fully human and was often gracious and generous. She made the best pot roast in three kingdoms. But on the second and fourth Thursdays of every month, her ogre-ish tendencies rose to the surface and she sought blood. Human, preferably.

As misfortune would have it, I happened to be born on

a second Thursday. Luckily, as soon as I emitted my first wail I was whisked to safety and guarded over by the servants of the castle, all of whom had been entrusted to keep our family's secret.

I was not a handsome baby. I had one blond hair, which curled straight up on my head like a pig's tail. My skin had an odd carrot-colored tint to it, which the castle doctor promised my parents would fade in time. It was actually fortunate for me that I wasn't an example of physical beauty, since Mother banned anything of beauty from the castle. The pages, stewards, chamberlains, ladies-in-waiting, stable boys, and the cook (*especially* the cook) were all of the sort who were unlikely to find marriage partners.

It wasn't that Mother was unattractive herself and didn't want to be outshined. In fact, in the right light she was even quite pretty. Her loathing of beauty came from the ogre blood in her veins. She tried to overcome her intolerance and would occasionally allow her ladies-in-waiting to adorn her with a sparkly gown of colorful satin damask, only to rip it off after ten minutes and replace it with her usual drab brown flax dress. The only colorful object in the whole castle was a painting in the library of a girl reading on the grass. Apparently Mother had tried to remove it from the wall when she first married Father, but it was stuck there permanently. The castle carpenters and masons could not make it budge. The only way to get it down would have been to dismantle the entire wall. Mother grudgingly allowed it to stay, but it had to be covered each time she entered the library.

The townspeople loved Mother for her unglamorous ways, believing that she dressed in such a plain style to prove that she was not above them. She was the most popular queen since Queen Melinda, a hundred years back. Melinda's portrait hung in the Great Hall along with all the royal portraits dating back nearly a thousand years — none of them as colorful (and therefore offensive to Mother) as the painting in the library. As an infant, I was brought before them and told by my father that becoming a king is a position one earns, not inherits. When one family tree dies out, then the castle goes to the most deserving young man of the noble families. Queen Melinda and her husband, King Bertram, apparently died without a son to inherit their kingdom, although when I was tucked in at night I was often told stories of an old legend about Melinda's missing daughter. I never paid much attention. After all, what cared I of princesses who lived a hundred years ago? I would inherit our kingdom when Father passed away, just as he had from his own father. My future was set. All I had to do was remember to stay clear of Mother on the second and fourth Thursdays of the month. How hard could that be?

CHAPTER THREE

～ Princess Rose ～

One day when I was two, Mama and I were skipping through the gardens, enjoying the warm breezes of spring. I had learned to walk early, due to a combination of the fairies' gifts of gracefulness and intelligence. It seemed obvious to me that I should get around much easier on two legs, rather than crawling on my hands and knees. Thus, by eight months I was as sturdy as a child twice my age. By a year, I could skip and twirl and run.

So there we were, just skipping along in our matching purple dresses, smelling the roses, when I reached out and grabbed one. "Look, Mama, a rose, the same as me!" (Oh, yes, I could speak clearly as well. I could also tap-dance, sing opera, and play a waltz on the piano, flute, and viola.)

"Rose!" Mama yelled in a panic. She held out a trembling hand. "Give me the flower, please."

Somehow I had angered Mama. Unused to hearing anything other than praise for my actions, I quickly handed over the rose. As I did, I felt a slight sting on my thumb. I held my thumb up. I had never seen my own blood before. I had seen scraped knees on the children in town, and once Papa had been wounded when a hawk landed on his head during a hunt, but I had never seen blood this fresh and bright. The red droplet on my thumb both fascinated and scared me. "Look, Mama, I'm bleeding."

The color drained from her face. She grabbed me and hugged me so tight I almost couldn't breathe. A moment later she pulled back and looked at me. "You're still awake!" she exclaimed. "Oh, thank goodness!"

I was very confused. "I don't understand," I said. I may have been smart, but mostly my intelligence fell into the "book smart" category. Except for the walking and talking, most of my knowledge was of the sort that allowed me to distinguish the varieties of birds that lived on our land, or how many eggs you were left with if you started with ten, ate three, and then the chicken laid two more. The ways of grown-ups were something I could not grasp.

Mama bent down and took my hands in hers. "Oh, darling, don't you know about the spindle? Don't you remember the old fairy's curse?"

I nodded. Of course I remembered. The story had been retold to me nearly every day by my nursemaid, Becca.

Becca was getting on in years and I never had the heart to tell her I'd already heard the story. "But what has that to do with the rose?"

Mama kissed my thumb where the blood had now dried. Her warm breath felt nice.

"I feared the first drop of blood would take you away from me," she said, wiping a tear from the corner of her eye.

"But a thorn is not a spindle," I pointed out. (These were the kinds of things my supersmartness allowed me to recognize.)

She nodded. "I know. But I am not sure how specific the fairy's curse actually is. Perhaps any pointy object could do the same job as the spindle."

I thought about this, then grinned. "But it didn't. I'm not even remotely sleepy."

Mama gave me another hug. "No, it did not," she agreed. "But perhaps Lady Luck smiled upon us this time. I shall still feel better if we remove anything pointy from the castle."

So Mama hid anything that might possibly be sharp enough to make me bleed, including hairpins, combs, toothpicks, and bales of hay. The cows and horses were forced to eat only oats. After a week, Papa threw down his spoon at supper and said, "I cannot eat roast duck with a spoon! I demand a fork!"

Mama pushed her unkempt hair out of her eyes and

nodded wearily. She knew when a battle wasn't worth fighting. Plus, she was tired of having spinach stuck in her teeth.

The pointy objects were allowed back, but now a twenty-four-hour watch had been placed upon my head. I was never without Becca or one of the other ladies-in-waiting. I didn't mind. The extra protection made me feel loved and protected, but I couldn't help wondering if I was still in danger. I did not want to live my whole life in fear. One morning when I was six and had a rare moment to myself in the garden, I accidentally-on-purpose scraped my finger along the bark of a tree until it bled a little bit. I figured if the curse kicked in, then at least it would be over with. But I did not fall asleep for a hundred years. All I did was ruin my favorite white gown when I wiped my finger on it. Mama grounded me for a fortnight, but I think she was relieved, too. I was still watched all the time, but we all breathed a little easier.

CHAPTER FOUR

⊱ The Prince ⊰

As I grew, the rest of my hair came in and the carrot color faded from my skin. I was growing more handsome by the day. This worried my father, but Mother never seemed to notice. I was an easy child, never requiring much. Mother once said I could entertain myself for hours with two bricks and a bucket of molasses. Fortunately Mother did not mind a messy child, since more likely than not I had dirt in my hair and molasses on my chin by the time I went to bed.

It was hard to keep help at the castle, because the staff would quite often disappear under mysterious circumstances. Word got around. Since my chamberlains and nursemaids were always quitting (or worse), I was left to Mother's care much of the time. She kept me by her side when she went into town to bring alms to the poor. The townsfolk oohed and aahed at me and tickled me under the chin. Mother seemed pleased. She even sat me on her lap and combed out the tangles in my hair when they got so bad I couldn't see.

But on a certain fourth Thursday, everything changed. I

had recently turned seven. I was supposed to spend the day with Percival, a boy I did not much care for due to his being kind of sneaky and always wanting to steal sweets from the pantry. But his father was one of Father's barons, and I often got stuck playing with him. At the last minute his mother came down with a cold and I was disinvited. Father thought I was a safe distance away, so he went hunting for stag with his friends.

Unguarded, I wandered out into the garden. Since the gardener wasn't allowed to plant any pretty flowers, most of the garden was used for herbs and vegetables. But I had discovered a single flower bed, deep into the garden, where roses still grew. The path there was narrow, and I don't think anyone but me ever visited. Once far enough away from Mother's ears, I began to hum a little tune. I swore I heard a voice humming along with me, but whenever I looked around, no one was there. On my way to my secret rose-bush, I stopped at the swing that had hung from the old oak tree for generations. I climbed up on it and imagined my father and grandfather swinging from the same spot when they were boys. Below me was a small, cracked fountain with a marble mermaid on the top. Father said water used to come out of her mouth. Mother said the gurgling sounded too much like music, so it had been drained long ago.

The mermaid looked sad, and I did not want to ruin my

good mood, so I moved on. When I reached the rosebush, I bent down and rubbed the petals between my fingers. I smiled when I saw the stain they left behind. Even though I spent much of my time alone, I was not unhappy. I played with the petals for a few more minutes, then realized that since no one was watching me, I might as well try to find the old building I had heard whisperings of. Supposedly the mysterious building was so overgrown with ivy and leaves as to be virtually indistinguishable from the forest around it. No one knew exactly where it was. The servants heard from their grandparents, who had heard from *their* parents, that the building was haunted and that no good would come to anyone who went near it. But I had a mother who was part ogre; I was not scared of a ghost.

"Don't move," a voice growled from behind me. I froze in my tracks, one foot already in the forest, one still on the lawn. I had never heard a voice like that. Had a strange man wandered onto the grounds? Where were the castle guards? Surely we still had some guards.

I slowly turned around, and let out a sigh of relief when I saw Mother standing there. I smiled and reached out to her. But she did not embrace me. I could see her shaking as she spoke.

"Run into the woods. NOW!"

Her eyes, usually a light brown, were now as black as my

nightmares. I ran. I ran farther into the woods than I'd ever run, not paying the slightest attention to where I was going. Squirrels darted out of my way. Startled birds filled the air. Eventually I realized no one was behind me. Mother had controlled her ogre urges to keep me safe. I leaned against a tree, panting hard. The tree suddenly gave way, and I fell backward and landed in a thick brush. What I thought was a tree had actually been a huge overgrowth of vines and leaves. I tried to stand, but my feet were stuck.

I wrenched my feet free and took a closer look at my surroundings. A stone wall was barely visible through layers of vines and entwined branches. I had found it! The mysterious building! I scratched away at the thick growth, but it held firm. I pushed harder, but it did not budge. The hunting bugle rang through the forest and I jumped back, almost falling again. Father would be very worried if he knew what had happened today. I needed to get back to my bedchambers before running into either parent.

The very top of the castle tower was visible from where I stood, so I knew which way to head. Luckily Mother was still out hunting, so I made it safely to my room and pushed the dresser in front of the door. At suppertime, one of the maids came to fetch me and escorted me down the back stairway, to the private dining room, which is where Father and I always ate on the second and fourth Thursdays.

Father was there when I arrived. "Did you have a nice time at Percival's?" he asked, polishing off his second mug of mead.

Unsure what to say but hesitant to lie, I merely coughed.

"Good," he said, seemingly satisfied. "I think you need to spend more time with boys your age."

I nodded. When you're a prince who will someday be their ruler, the other boys aren't very anxious to be your pal. And since the staff knew better than to bring their kids to the castle, I didn't have any real friends.

That night at five past midnight, I heard my door open. I knew it was Mother. She came to check on me every second and fourth Thursday at this time. Usually I didn't even fully wake up, but tonight was different. I quickly sat up in bed. She sat down next to me. I stiffened for a second. When I saw her hurt expression, I felt bad and moved closer.

"I won't always be able to control it like today," she said sadly, not meeting my eyes. "That was too close a call."

I nodded.

"Let us not speak of it anymore," she said, fluffing my pillow. "I expect never to see you on those days again."

"I promise," I said. She kissed me on the forehead, which is something she had only done a handful of times in my memory. It might have been worth the day's scare.

For a few days Mother avoided me. She claimed she was

too busy to take me into town with her or to play a game. Perhaps she believed it was easier on both of us this way. I knew she was embarrassed, but I wished she wouldn't be. We can't help our own natures.

Even though things settled back into their routine, my relationship with her was never the same. With Father off doing kingly stuff most of the time, and the servants never staying long enough for me to get to know any of them, I was truly on my own now. I was still only seven years old.

CHAPTER FIVE

~ Princess Rose ~

You Are Cordially Invited to the Castle
Princess Rose Turns Eight!
All Your Slumber Needs Shall Be Accommodated
Seven o'clock in the eve until ten o'clock in the morn
R.S.V.P. to Queen Melinda

I was so very excited. My first slumber party! Another year had come and gone, and I hadn't managed to become impaled on a spindle. Hurrah!

This year my guests included four girls from the most important families in the kingdom — Meggin, Clarissa, Tabitha, and Bethany — and a girl from town named Sara whom I had befriended the past year when I'd gone with Mama to drop off some clothes. Papa had kept his promise and always made certain the townsfolk had enough to wear. He imported the clothes from all over, and then Mama herself (and her staff of twenty) delivered them. Sara had been the one to open the door of their small farmhouse when Mama knocked. Sara was so surprised to see the queen that she fell over backward and knocked over a bowl of cabbage soup that her younger sister was about to set down on the table. Sara had strands of green cabbage dripping from her hair, which was the color of strawberries. I laughed and helped her up from the ground.

The next time we went to deliver clothes, Sara taught me how to milk a cow. Before I could touch it, Mama first had to make sure there were no pointy parts on the animal. Old habits die hard. Sara said she could hear the town crier now: **Hear ye, hear ye, our beloved Princess Rose has been brought down by a common farm cow! More information when she wakes up!** Sara and I laughed till tears ran down our cheeks. Mama didn't think it was very amusing.

Promptly at seven o'clock, the girls began to arrive with their overnight bags. Their parents or servants dropped them off. Some stayed to chat with my parents, who assured them that we would be supervised at all times. Of course we would — when was I ever *not* supervised? Sure, there were some hidden passageways in the castle that I had yet to explore, and there might be a cute page or two that we could spy on, and perhaps I knew where the cook hid the sweets in the back corner of the pantry behind the milled wheat, but none of that was on our agenda. Our agenda had only one item on it.

Makeovers!

The last to arrive was Sara. She and her mother did not have a carriage, so they walked up to the castle. Sara didn't have a father. She never spoke of what happened to him. The porter had the guest list, so he did not give them any trouble crossing the moat. Sara and her mother lingered inside the gate, clearly a bit overwhelmed by the majesty of our home. I had worried a bit that Sara might stand out, but fortunately since all of the girls lived close enough that they had to get their clothes from my father, everyone was dressed in similar summer shifts. Mine had an extra bit of embroidery along the bottom.

The other girls began whispering when Sara arrived, which I did not think was very kind. So I looped my arm in hers and brought her over to the group. I made the introductions, and then we all hurried up the winding stone staircase to my bedroom suite. Six ladies-in-waiting hurried after us.

Bethany stopped halfway up the stairs and whispered, "Rose, why are they following us?"

"What do you mean?"

She gestured behind us at the ladies-in-waiting. "I thought we were going to your room to do makeovers."

"We are."

She sighed. "In *private*."

I had grown so accustomed to being watched over that it didn't bother me anymore. Most of the time I simply forgot anyone else was in the room. I looked around at the other girls, and they were all nodding. Even Sara.

"They won't bother us, I promise. It's not as if they're spying on us."

The girls looked skeptical but continued following me upstairs. When we got into my suite, the ladies-in-waiting gathered in the sitting room. We all jumped up onto my four-poster bed.

"Wow," Sara said, her eyes large as she looked around the room. "Is all of this yours? This whole bed and everything?"

I nodded, recalling that she had to share a bed with her sister. To change the subject, I said, "Let's see what everyone brought!"

With a collective squeal, the girls emptied the contents of their bags onto the bed—jars of makeup and brushes and tubes of lip paint, baubles of all colors and shapes, feathered caps, pots of glitter, wigs, and butterfly pins for our hair. Clarissa even brought a corset she had "borrowed" from her older sister. Someone banged the knocker on my door and we jumped. I had requested Papa send up a page with six full-length mirrors, and could I help it if the cute page was the only one working tonight? When he came in the room, the girls giggled some more. Sara blushed deeply when he bowed to her and said, "How do you do, madam?"

"He likes you!" Bethany shrieked.

The ladies-in-waiting came hurrying in from the next room. "We heard a scream," Becca said, an edge of panic to her voice. "Is everything all right?"

"Yes, Becca," I assured her. "We're only having fun."

Becca didn't look amused. She glanced hard at the mess on the bed, then led the ladies back into the sitting room.

Tabitha reached for a pot of blusher and said, "It would drive me batty if I always had people looking over my shoulder."

"Me, too," the others said. I was surprised. Having so many people looking after my best interests just made me feel that much more loved.

"Shall we go to the mirrors?" Sara suggested. I was grateful to her for taking the focus off me.

I placed one of my feather pillows in front of each mirror. Then we each carried over an armful of supplies.

For the next half-hour, we proceeded to make ourselves over. I became a blond. Sara became a brunette. Bethany painted her lips bright crimson. Meggin helped Tabitha lace up the corset. Tabitha had to wrap her arms around a bedpost to keep from falling over. It made her look deformed!

We all got a good laugh and then Meggin unlaced it for her. Another knock came. This time it was my parents.

"Don't mind us," they said, taking seats on the cushioned bench across from us. "We'll just watch. Why, we would hardly recognize you girls, all outfitted up like that."

The girls smiled politely, but it wasn't the same with Mama and Papa there. Clarissa fastened a butterfly pin in her hair, but when it fell out she didn't bother to fix it. After a few minutes she said, "I am quite tired, Your Highnesses. Perhaps you could show us to our rooms?"

I opened my mouth to point out that the eve was still young, but all the other girls except for Sara jumped up so quickly to join her that I fell silent.

"Certainly," Mama said, not picking up on the girls' displeasure with the situation. One by one they gathered up their belongings and filed out. They each mouthed the word *sorry* as they left. I wasn't sure if they were apologizing for cutting the party short, or whether they were saying they felt sorry for me. I didn't know which was worse. I pulled off my blond wig and let it dangle in my hand. I wanted to run and hide. Last year while helping Papa take inventory of the wine cellar I had discovered the perfect nook in the corner. On the rare moments I was alone, I hid there with a book, a candle, and some of Cook's special plum cakes.

Besides two ladies-in-waiting, Sara was the only one still

in my room. "You'll be in my favorite guest quarters next door," I told her, staring down at the circular pattern on the rug. Once she left, I would pretend to sleep and then head down to the cellar.

"If it wouldn't be too much of an inconvenience," Sara said softly, "I'd rather stay in here with you. I'm so used to sharing a bed with my sister, I don't think I would slumber if left alone. And your bed is so big you could fit ten of me and twenty of my sister and still not notice we were there."

I looked up in surprise. I could not wipe the smile off my face. "Fifty of you and a hundred of your sister!" I replied.

"Two hundred!" she shouted.

"THREE HUNDRED!" I yelled.

I decided right then and there to give Sara all the presents the other girls brought me, which sat unopened downstairs. Sara had already given me the best gift I could have asked for. "Sara?" I said as she began wiping the bright lip paint off her lips with a piece of damp cloth.

"Yes?"

"Do you think I'm quite strange?"

"Of course," she replied. "That's why we're friends. I'm strange, too."

"No, I don't mean strange *good*, I mean strange *bad*. Because of them?" I tilted my head into the sitting room where the last two ladies-in-waiting sat.

She did not answer right away. Then she said, "Well, I do not think it is the customary thing, but your parents have good reason to worry after you. And to be truthful, with my father gone and my mother working all hours of the day and night, I wouldn't mind it if people looked after me every now and again."

"I shall look after you," I declared.

She smiled. "You will need those seven-league boots for that."

Sara had once told me a tale about magical boots that allowed the wearer to cover seven leagues in just one step. She figured if I owned them, I could reach her house from the castle in a little more than three steps.

It turned out I did not need magic boots to look after Sara. A few weeks after my birthday party, Sara learned that her mother was going to marry a blacksmith in another part of town. She was selling the farm and moving the family. The blacksmith had five children of his own, and the house was tiny. Sara was distraught.

I immediately asked Mama if Sara could stay with us. Mama said of course she could. But Sara insisted she could not simply be a guest. She wanted to be useful. So I said good-bye to long-suffering Becca, and hello to Sara, my new lady-in-waiting who also happened to be my best friend.

CHAPTER SIX

⤙ The Prince ⤚

At nine years old, my favorite food was roast mutton. For months I would eat nothing else. Having a hearty meat-eater for a son pleased Mother, but the kitchen staff was beginning to worry.

One night Father's trusted chamberlain was helping him prepare for bed and muttered something under his breath. When Father asked him to repeat it, he at first refused. Father asked again. It is impossible to say no to my father twice, so the chamberlain was forced to repeat his comment. "All I said, sir — and forgive me my boldness —was to wonder aloud about your son's, ah, eating habits."

Father looked surprised. "Many children have strange tastes. Why, when I was the Prince's age, I would eat only quail eggs and strawberry jam."

"I am sure you are right, Your Highness. It is probably only a phase. Let us put on your nightclothes now."

The chamberlain held up Father's dressing gown, but

Father narrowed his eyes and said, "You do not believe it is a phase, do you?"

"I am sure I don't know, Your Highness," said the chamberlain, no doubt wishing he had never mentioned anything.

"You think he may be part ogre, like the Queen."

The chamberlain chewed on his lip and didn't answer. Father sighed and sat down on the edge of his bed. "I admit, I have wondered the same thing." He put his head in his hands. The chamberlain awkwardly patted Father on the shoulder.

"Er, it will be all right, Your Highness. I am sure your first theory was correct. So the boy likes mutton? A lot. So what? I haven't seen any other ogre-ish tendencies in him."

"Nor have I," Father said, raising his head slightly. "But how can we be certain?"

The chamberlain paced the room, unused to being taken into the King's confidence in this way. "We can devise a test," he suggested. "Although we don't know what day, or days, of the month his ogre-ish blood will rise to the surface — not that I'm saying it will — but if it does, we need to be prepared ahead of time."

"What kind of test?" Father asked miserably.

The chamberlain shook his head. "I am not sure. Perhaps you could consult with the castle chaplain? He could pray on it."

Father stood up and clasped his chamberlain on the forearm. "That is an excellent idea. I shall do that first thing in the morning."

The chamberlain nodded and began dressing Father in his nightclothes.

"And by the way," Father continued, "you're fired for being so impertinent as to speak to me about my son."

The chamberlain gaped and turned white.

"Ha-ha, just kidding, old man," Father said. "You're not fired."

(Besides my mom's "issues," my dad's "sense of humor" was also why it was hard to keep good help around.)

The next morning Father went directly to the castle chaplain, and together they devised a test for me. They found as many strangers as they could, and each day invited a different one to have lunch with me and Father out on the Great Lawn. Mother always had committee meetings at lunchtime (she was very active in the community, part of her whole "beloved by the masses" thing), so Father knew the newcomers to the castle would be safe.

I was so thrilled to be spending time with Father that it never even dawned on me to suspect anything. As the month was winding down, Father had run out of strangers and had to invite the same ones back again. Even though I loved spending time with Father and felt important for the first time in my life, the lunches were deadly boring. By the time the guests started to repeat, I tried desperately to get out of going. Father agreed that all I had to do was show up and shake the person's hand. Then I could be on my way. This was fine with me. Not that I had any grand plans for my free time. I longed to immerse myself in my studies, but no tutors stayed around long enough for me to get through a whole geography or history lesson. Most children would probably be pleased with that, but I was often bored. I wanted to learn about the outside world, but no one was there to teach me. I spent much time in the aviary with the falconer, who let me feed the birds that accompanied Father when he went out hunting. Even though they had very sharp beaks, they never bit me. The falconer said I was his favorite visitor. I happened to know I was also the falconer's *only* visitor, but I appreciated him trying to make me feel good.

On the last day of the month, with the last lunch a few hours behind us, Father found me playing with my toy soldiers in the library. He sat down next to me on the floor, something I can't ever remember him doing, and said, "Congratulations, my boy! You don't have a drop of ogre blood in you!"

I stared at him. "What do you mean?"

Then he told me about the test, and how I had passed by apparently not attacking any of the guests.

"But why did you think I might have gotten some of Mother's ogre blood? Have I done something terrible?" My heart began to race at the thought of it. Perhaps I did horrible things and didn't remember them! Why had I never considered that I might have inherited her ogre ways?

"Oh, no, nothing like that," Father assured me. "Actually, it was the mutton."

"The mutton? What mutton?"

"All the mutton you eat at every meal. We thought perhaps the fact that you were drawn to such a meat-filled meal indicated you had a thirst for . . . for . . . other meaty things."

I shuddered at the thought. "To be honest, I am getting very tired of mutton. I was going to ask the cook to make me something different, like quail eggs."

"Excellent idea," Father said. "I'll alert him myself."

I thought about all those special lunches. I couldn't believe all the trouble they went to. "Did you ever consider just bringing me something of beauty? Flowers? A nice painting or two? If I liked it, that would have proved I wasn't an ogre."

"Hmm," Father said. "Hadn't thought of that. Sure would have saved me from a lot of boring meals."

"You thought they were boring, too?" I asked.

He smiled and tussled my hair. "Of course. I don't know

how your mother does it, all those luncheon meetings with the same groups of women." He shuddered. "It would drive me mad."

I had a question I'd wanted to ask him for years. Considering this was the longest conversation the two of us had probably ever had, I figured it was the right time to ask it.

"Father?" I began.

"Yes?"

"Do you ever talk to Mother about, you know, what it's like for her? The whole part-ogre thing?"

Father shook his head. "When she first told me, I asked some questions, but she never wanted to talk about it. She's ashamed. I told her that no one can help what's in their blood. It is not their choice."

"That's how I feel, too!" I said eagerly. "I don't blame her. I just wish she didn't shut me out so much."

Father nodded. "Me, too, son, but that's just the way she is. It doesn't mean she doesn't love you." He reddened a bit as he said the last part. We were not a family that tossed the *love* word around in casual conversation.

I wasn't so sure of Mother's love, but I said, "I know."

Father uncrossed his legs creakily and stood up. Before he left the room he said, "A new page is transferring to our castle tomorrow. He's about your age. How about he becomes your personal attendant? You could use a close friend around here."

I nodded. A friend wasn't the same as a parent, but I'd take it. "Father?" I called out, surprising even myself. He turned around and stuck his head back in the room.

"Father, how come I don't have a name?"

He didn't answer for a moment, then said, "When you were born, we wanted to make sure things were going to, shall we say, work out. Everyone simply referred to you as the Prince, and eventually that became your name."

"That's what I thought," I replied. "I just wanted to be certain."

I went back to setting the toy soldiers up for battle. I thought Father had left but then heard, "Would you like a name?"

Startled, I dropped the soldier in my hand. It hit the rug with barely a sound. I nodded.

"How about you pick your own?" Father said. "Come to me when you've chosen." With that, he left me.

I was quite taken aback. It is not every day one is told they may pick their own name. What a huge responsibility! Mortimer? Octavian? Rex? How would I choose? By dinner-time (quail eggs and strawberry jam, which was delicious) I had landed on Rhyan. A solid, strong-sounding name. By dessert, I had changed it to James. By the time I climbed into bed, it was Lucas for sure. When I woke up, I couldn't even remember why I liked Lucas. I obviously wasn't ready to saddle myself with a name yet. Instead of me finding my name, my name would just have to find me.

CHAPTER SEVEN

∽ Princess Rose ↶

I laced up my ballet slippers and flexed my ankles in preparation for my performance. Each year since I could walk — which you recall was at quite a tender age — Mama and Papa had invited the lords and ladies of the kingdom to the castle to watch me sing and dance and play musical instruments. My parents figured that since the fairies were kind enough to bless me with these gifts, I owed it to high society to share them. I never gave much thought as to whether I enjoyed these performances. They took almost no effort, since everything came naturally to me. I knew it made my parents proud, and that was enough for me.

My eleventh birthday had just passed. I had long ago given up on having parties. I was happy to celebrate with my parents and Sara, who had become more like a sister to me than a lady-in-waiting. She went to visit her real sister, Amelia, every month at the blacksmith's house, and Amelia often came to the castle, too. In fact, she was in the audience tonight. The cute page I had admired when I was younger (who went by the name of Clive) had become a squire. I saw him every now and then practicing with the knights. Sara wouldn't admit it, but she lingered by the thick glass windows whenever he was jousting out on the Great Lawn.

Mama had ordered red velvet drapes, which she'd fashioned into a makeshift curtain. I would stand behind the curtain, and then when it was time for my next piece, the curtains would open dramatically and I would begin my routine. It all came across as quite professional. I had already sung ten minutes of an opera that night as my opening act. I was glad that part was over. I liked singing little wordless songs as I strolled through the gardens or helped Cook bake her delectable desserts, but I could not stand opera. It was very odd to be so excellent at something that I didn't even enjoy.

The curtains drew apart and I began my ballet dance. My mind was utterly detached as I flitted and fluttered across the stage (really some boards of wood the castle carpenter had nailed together, which caused my mother to nearly faint until he assured her the pointy ends of the nails were underneath the stage and would not harm me).

At appropriate intervals my arms arched upward and out to the side like butterfly wings, and my neck tilted back so my hair flowed down like a sheet of silk. I closed my eyes and twirled on my tiptoes, never losing my balance. The crowd was hushed, watching me. Meanwhile, I was thinking about the adorable little snail I had found on my window ledge that morning. What a trip he must have had to crawl all the way from the ground, three stories below! I had just determined to call him Rex when the song ended and the applause began. For the first time, I felt a bit guilty about accepting such adulation. For truly it was almost none of my doing.

Sara helped me change out of my ballet outfit and into a long yellow gown for the last part of the concert. "You were excellent," she whispered as she fastened the bow behind my back.

"Thanks," I said, not really feeling it.

"Is something the matter?" she asked.

There was no keeping anything from Sara. She could read me like a book. But I wasn't quite sure what I was feeling so I shook my head. "It is time for me to go back on," I said.

I played an original medley on the piano, then moved to the flute, and finally the viola. The piece would have sounded even better had all three instruments been played at the same time, but the fairy's gift stopped short of giving me that ability. This time after the usual round of applause (and a standing ovation and an armful of thorn-free roses) I felt tears prick my eyes. No doubt the audience thought they were tears of joy and gratitude. They were not. I felt hollow inside.

That night after Sara hung up my gown in the wardrobe, she sat down on the edge of my bed. "Speak," she instructed.

I pretended not to know what she meant. How could I explain that I felt like I had not earned any of the praise that was constantly heaped upon me? My tutors always gave me the highest marks in our little class, even though the other students worked much harder at getting the correct answers. My gracefulness gave me excellent posture, so I always walked taller than the others, which made me seem haughty. How could I complain about the bounty of gifts heaped upon me, when Sara had so little? How could I explain that no one — not even me — knew the real me, the person I would have become without the fairies' help?

"May I take a guess at what is troubling you?" Sara asked.

I sighed and nodded.

"Do you not like being the center of attention on that stage? Do all those eyes make you uncomfortable?"

I shook my head. That part of it had never bothered me. I was so used to being watched. Besides my special situation, a princess is going to be looked at wherever she goes. It comes with the territory.

"Were your ballet slippers too tight and squeezing your toes?"

I laughed a little. "No, they were fine."

"Did that nobleman in the front row have such bad body odor that you couldn't concentrate up there?"

I laughed harder. The man had desperately been in need of a bath, but I shook my head.

Sara threw up her arms. "I give up, then."

"I am fine, truly," I insisted. "I shall see you in the morning for our usual walk."

"You're the boss," she said, heading off to her own room next door. She had learned to get used to having a bed to herself.

We both smiled at her parting words. We knew exactly who the real boss was. Sara still watched me carefully according to Mama's orders, but she gave me much more freedom than any of my other ladies-in-waiting had. For that I was grateful. I climbed under the blanket and decided I would take it upon myself to discover the real Rose. I had no idea how, but something had to change or I was in danger of losing myself completely.

CHAPTER EIGHT

← The Prince →

The new page at the castle — Jonathan — became not only my trusted companion but also my teacher, woodland guide, and protector. He and I were the same age, born only days apart, but he had seen more of the world than I imagined existed. By the time we were twelve, he had taught me how to fish, how to figure out which berries were safe to eat, and which would turn your insides to mush, how to use mud and straw to build a perfectly sturdy hut, and how to best avoid Mother on the second and fourth Thursdays.

The reason he spent so much time educating me on the ways of the wild was that I tended to run away often. The first time was when I was ten. Mother had forgotten to wipe the blood from her chin at breakfast, following her "meal" the night before. (Luckily, I realized it was not human blood.) For the first time in my life, I felt revulsion toward her. This is not a nice feeling to have toward my own mother, who, truly, had never done me any harm. I felt so terrible that I knew I could not stay. I put on my sturdy leather boots, took an old potato sack from the pantry, stuffed it with a few tunics, a cloak, some apples, and a chunk of hard cheese, and took off for parts unknown. I did not tell anyone I was leaving. Jonathan had been with us not quite a year at that point, and I, being so unfamiliar with friendships, had been too shy to exchange anything other than pleasantries.

With a glance behind me to make sure I wasn't being followed, I ran across the Great Lawn into the woods. Once I knew I was out of sight of the castle, I slowed down. The woods were nice and cool. I loved how the tops of the trees met across the paths, making a canopy for me to walk under. One good thing about not studying life in books was that it forced me to pay more attention to my surroundings. I loved being out in nature and watching the animals and the bugs and even the grass growing. Father caught me once, just lying on the lawn, alternately watching the grass and the formations of the clouds. He asked me what I was doing, so I told him. He raised his brows and muttered, "My boy is an odd duck."

I did not know what he meant by that, so I took it as a compliment and kept studying nature in all its forms. Even in the dense woods alone, I felt very confident. Before I knew it, I found myself in front of the mysterious overgrown building. The sun was still high in the sky, so I decided to walk fully around the building to get an idea of its shape. I first munched on an apple for sustenance, then left the sack behind so I would know where I started from.

I was still unable to break through the vines to see any more than the occasional glimpse of the gray stone walls. Here and there I saw a glint of a windowpane. Every time I turned a corner I expected the building to end, but it did not. It was much more massive than I had ever imagined. When I finally returned to my starting point, an hour had passed. How was it possible that such a huge structure could be on the grounds of our castle without anyone knowing what it truly was or how to get inside? I backed up a few yards. From that distance, the building looked like no more than a clump of trees and leaves. I could see that if one wasn't looking directly at it, one could miss it entirely. I felt a little tingle as I approached it again. I wondered if something magical had taken place on this spot. There was something slightly otherworldly about it. I still believed in magic and fairies, although I had no proof of their existence, only old fables.

There was something sort of familiar about the place, too. I could not put my finger on it. Now that I had a sense of its shape, I felt like I had been there before, and not just the time I had run to escape Mother. It was getting darker now, and the air had cooled by at least ten degrees. I affixed my cloak over my shoulders and struggled with the clasp.

Normally a chamberlain would have dressed me (when one bothered to show up to work), but I liked being able to do things on my own. I envied how Jonathan seemed to be able to tackle any task. I knew that in order to be a knight he had to work very hard to master many skills. It appeared all I had to do to be a prince was not get eaten. I doubted that anyone at the castle even knew I had gone.

I gathered some fallen leaves into a pile and burrowed inside. I finished off the other apple and all the cheese and wondered what to do next. With dusk came the animals who had hidden during the sunlight hours. An owl hooted so loudly I was sure it was right next to me. Normally I found the sounds of the animals soothing. Now, however, they sounded unfamiliar and even predatory. My stomach rumbled. I was used to Cook's five-course meals. If I strained really hard, I could almost smell the food cooking from where I was standing. I let my mind wander over all the possible items on tonight's menu. By the time I started picturing peach cobbler with a mixture of Cook's special spices on top, I had to forcibly hold myself down. I had not thought of how long I planned to run away for, but there was no way I was giving up after only one afternoon.

An hour passed. Then another. It was now pitch black. The sliver of moon between the tops of the trees was barely enough to allow me to see my hand in front of my face. I began to hum the tune of one of Father's favorite songs. He always requested it of the traveling minstrels. It was an old song, and no minstrel sang it exactly the same way. The one thing the versions had in common, though, was the part about a sad princess who had a long time to wait for her prince. I never gave the words much thought, but it had a sweet tune.

I must have fallen asleep, because the next thing I knew it was dawn. Most of the leaves had fallen off me, and there were fresh tracks right next to me. They could have been from a coyote or a mountain lion. I was very lucky the beast had left me alone. As my stomach growled again in protest, it occurred to me that I had not planned very well. Next time I wouldn't make the same mistakes.

Wearily, I headed back toward the castle. Before I was too far from the mystery building, I turned to give it one last glance. It hit me like a bolt of lightning why the place felt so familiar. It was an exact replica of our own castle! Or perhaps our own castle was an exact replica of it? Surely this one must be ancient to be so fully covered by the forest. Perhaps Father knew when our castle was built. I hurried back toward the path that would lead me home. Halfway there, Jonathan appeared, hands on his hips.

"Were you sleeping on the forest floor all night?" he asked.

I nodded. "I put some leaves on top of me."

"I see you managed not to get eaten by a wolf," he said.

"That is true, I was not eaten by a wolf. There were some tracks near me when I awoke, but I was fine."

He shook his head. "You must have a fairy godmother. The forest is full of animals who could eat you in one bite. Speaking of food, did you have enough?"

At this point in the conversation, I did not feel like revealing any more of my failures, nor did I want to tell him about the old castle, so I just shrugged. I began to walk again, and he fell in alongside me.

"So," he said, "am I to expect you will be running away often?"

"I would say that's a good possibility," I answered honestly.

"Well, in that case I'm going to have to teach you better survival skills. You were lucky this time."

"Fine," I replied, trying not to show how excited I was. I was finally going to learn something!

Thus our lessons, and our friendship, began in earnest. After admonishing me for my actions, my parents paid extra attention to me. That lasted approximately a day and a half, and then things were back to normal: visits to the aviary in the morning, followed by lessons with Jonathan in the afternoons. Father claimed not to know exactly when our castle was built but said he believed it was sometime between the days of King Bertram and our family's reign. When I inquired as to why they had to build a new castle when most castles could last a thousand years, Father shrugged and said he had to meet with the bailiff to discuss some important kingly business, so I had better be going.

The next time I ran away, a few months later, I was much better prepared and lasted three full nights in the woods. I was still no closer to getting into the old castle, even with the tools I had brought. Those vines were seemingly impenetrable. It was a mystery, all right — a mystery I was getting more and more anxious to get to the bottom of.

CHAPTER NINE

～ Princess Rose ～

Project: Discover the Real Rose
The first thing I did was to make a list of the things I knew I could do well.

1. Sing (anything, like a songbird)
2. Dance (ballet, tap, ballroom)
3. Play music (there is no instrument I cannot master)
4. Be graceful (I never, ever trip, including when I walk backward while blindfolded)
5. Be smart (I only have to glance at a page of a book and I can recite it a year later. My head is full of information I shall never, ever need to use.)
6. Be beautiful (long hair that never tangles, clear skin that never pimples, a pleasing aroma even when I don't bathe)

So now I knew my strengths. But my weaknesses? I had no idea. It took me some time to get up the nerve to find out what I could do on my own. I suppose I was afraid that without the magic gifts I was nothing at all.

When I turned thirteen I finally got up the nerve to tell Mama that I didn't want to do the annual performance anymore. I offered to still sing and dance for the family and invited guests on feast days.

"But why?" she asked, a look of concern flitting across her eyes. "Are you ill?" She reached out to rest the back of her hand against my forehead. "You do feel a bit warm. Shall I call the castle physician?"

"I'm not ill," I told her. "It is simply that . . . it is just that I . . . er . . ."

I still could not explain my real reasons, and thankfully she did not press me. I knew she was disappointed, but something had changed inside me. I was ready to face whatever disappointments or failures came my way. I needed to try things I had never attempted before. Things where the gifts would not give me an unfair advantage over others.

I spent the afternoon walking the complete length of the castle, inside and out. When Sara got tired, another lady-in-waiting took her place. I was pretending to do some sort of inventory of our belongings, but really I was watching everyone go about their daily business to see what interested me. I watched the carpenter fix a bench in the rectory, and the physician minister to a baron's son who had tripped while chasing a rooster. I clapped when the glassmaker completed a beautiful piece of stained glass that would replace a cracked piece in one of the upstairs windows. I shed a tear when a farmhand helped a cow to deliver a baby calf. That calf reminded me of myself. Born into a destiny it could not escape.

I stared at the tapestries that lined the hall walls and floors in the lower parts of the castle. The details were so intricate: the tiny blue eyes on the babies; the foam coming out of the mouths of the horses in battle. I could not imagine how anyone could create such a thing using only a needle and thread. Of course I did not know anyone who did *anything* with fabrics, seeing as I had never in my life so much as laid eyes on a spinning wheel or a loom or a needle.

I tasted the vegetable broth in the kitchen that would be part of that night's soup, and watched the squires as they raced one another on horseback as part of their daily exercises (Sara wasn't too tired of walking to come along with me on that one!). I watched the winemaker stomp on grapes with his bare feet and made a mental note not to have wine ever again. I even watched the dung cleaner clean the dung chutes. Needless to say, that was one area in which I did not feel the need to test my skills.

At the end of the day, I made a list of the tasks that interested me the most.

1. I love the tapestries, but since I dare not try to sew, I can do the next best thing and try my hand at painting.
2. I've always enjoyed helping Cook to make desserts, but all she ever lets me do is add a pinch of sugar here, a dollop of honey there. I should like to try making a whole meal for the family.
3. The squires looked so free and alive while on those horses. I should like to try riding. Mama is always afraid to let me, but I know how to be careful.

I waited patiently for Sara's day to visit her family, then had one of the coachmen take me into town to purchase art supplies. One of the other ladies-in-waiting would normally have accompanied me in Sara's absence, but I assured her the coachman would keep a very good eye on me.

I had no idea what I needed to buy, other than some paint and something to put it on. These items were not as easy to find as I would have hoped. It appeared the townsfolk did not have much leisure time to engage in the arts. I caused a bit of a stir by turning up unexpectedly at so many shops. The whole princess thing combined with the whole most-beautiful-girl-in-the-world thing made me quite a spectacle. Little children leaned out of their windows to see me. Shopkeepers tried hard to sell me things I did not need. Women stared admiringly at my clothes. Finally I wound up with a pallet, five jars of crushed pigment, oil to mix them with, three brushes of different sizes, an easel that folded up, and a small canvas stretched onto two pieces of wood.

I smuggled my goods back into the house. This was no easy task, either. As soon as I returned home, the questions began.

Mama: *Where did you go?*

Papa: *Whom were you with?*

Mama & Papa: *Are you all right?*

I told them I had gone into town to get supplies for an anniversary gift I was making for them. As soon as I said it, I knew I wasn't even lying. Mama said, "But our anniversary isn't for another ten months."

"Well, think upon it as a belated anniversary from the last one," I said, then hurried upstairs with my bundle wrapped up in my traveling cloak.

I knew my only alone-time would be at night, so directly after supper I told the newly returned Sara that I was turning in early. I managed to be in my room alone while there was still light in the sky. I set up the easel in front of the largest window and mixed my first jar of pigment. It was messier than I expected, and clumpier, too. But soon I had a pretty blue color with which to color the sky. I had decided to paint the garden in the courtyard below my window. That way I wouldn't have to go outside to do it. I had a perfect view from my room.

I did not know which brush to use, so I chose the smallest one. That turned out to be a mistake, since it was starting to get dark out and I had a lot more sky to paint. I switched to the largest brush, and that went much faster. It also used up more of the pigment, so I had to keep adding water to thin it out. The result was that the canvas looked like it was going to tear in a few places from being too wet.

It was now completely dark out, and I had to finish the sky from memory. I wanted to add a white cloud, but whenever I put the white pigment over the blue, it merely made a lighter blue. Clearly, this whole painting thing was much more complicated than it at first appeared. When Sara came in the next morning to awaken me, she asked, "What is that horrid odor?" Then she lifted one of my arms and took a quick sniff.

"Very funny," I said, pushing my arm back down. I had stashed my work-in-progress under the bed, out of sight from prying eyes. I hoped a corner wasn't sticking out, but I didn't dare look or Sara would immediately catch on. As I hurried to the bathing room I added, "I do not know of what odor you speak."

"Sure, you don't," she said, reaching into the wardrobe for my clothes. "I may not know what you're up to yet, but I'll find out."

I was in the middle of gargling with lemon water and pretended not to hear her.

The next night I tackled the garden. I mixed the rest of the pigments — red, green, yellow, and brown — but before I began to paint I used a charcoal pencil to first lightly outline the edges of the garden that separate each plant from its neighbor.

I started with the red roses, since they were, of course, my favorite flower. Even using the smallest brush, I found it hard to get the detail of the flowers quite right. The petals tended to blend into one another. The stems were easier. When I was finished with all the flowers, I took a few steps back to admire my work.

Hmm. Well. It was *colorful*. Perhaps that is the best thing I could say about it. I signed P.R. (for Princess Rose) in the lower right-hand corner, because I knew that was what artists did. I slid the painting under the bed to dry and washed out my jars and brushes, nearly staining the porcelain sink in the process. It took two hours of scrubbing with lye and sandpaper to get out the reddish color.

The next day I requested Mama, Papa, and Sara wait in my sitting room, facing the other way, while I prepared to show them what I had been working on. With their backs still turned, I unfolded the easel and set up the painting.

"You can turn around now," I announced.

At first no one said anything. Three jaws opened slightly, then promptly closed again.

"Um, what is it?" Papa asked, peering closely. "Is it a duck?"

"Hush," Mama said. "It's obvious. It's a bonnet."

"A bonnet!" I exclaimed. "Where do you see a bonnet?"

"Right there," Mama said, pointing to the garden patch. "That is clearly a bonnet, lying on the floor of a blue room."

"Is that what you see, Sara?" I asked.

"Uh, not exactly. I think it's a girl in a colorful dress. She's, er, reading a book? On the grass? Is it a self-portrait?"

I marched over to the painting and lifted it off the easel. "Happy anniversary," I told my parents happily.

"Er, thank you, darling, it's lovely whatever it is," Mama said, taking it from my arms. "We'll have to find a special place to hang this, won't we, Bertram?"

"Oh, yes, yes, a special place indeed."

That special place turned out to be a storage closet in the attic behind a dressmaker's mannequin that was no longer needed following my christening. It did not bother me, though. While it would have been nice to find something I had a natural (not fairy-given) talent for, I had found something I was NOT good at instead. For the first time in my life, I had failed.

It felt great!

CHAPTER TEN

The Prince

By the time I was fourteen, I had run away so many times, and returned safely each time, that my parents had given up trying to stop me. Father once asked me where it was that I went. I promised him it was not far, and that proved a good enough answer. I had moved on from one potato sack to three and now had the muscle to carry everything in one trip. I built two semipermanent forts in the woods, one that kept me cool in the summer and one warm in the winter. Both were in sight of the old castle and well hidden from my own.

On my last trip, I finally discovered something new. During my usual journey around the perimeter of the building, I found a button-sized area over one of the windows where the vines had separated slightly. It definitely hadn't been there on my last visit. The glass was clear and sharp, not dusty or cloudy like I would have thought after so many years without a cleaning. I could clearly see inside into what appeared to be a typical castle library. I saw a tall fireplace with a mantle, two large chairs, a few benches along the walls, a large rug on the floor. The odd thing about it was that the room seemed lit from within, which I knew was impossible. No oil lamp could possibly still work after so long a time. Yet there was so much light in the room it was as though daylight was shining right through the windows instead of being completely blocked from entering by the vines.

I couldn't take my eye away from that peephole. I had a feeling I was missing something important. I searched the room once more, trying to make out the objects on the shelves, hoping they might offer up some clues as to what had happened there. I saw a statue of a horse atop the man-tle, a pile of books on a side table, a painting on the wall of a girl reading on the grass, and a set of marble bookends in the shape of lions. My eyes swung back to the painting and locked.

I stared until my eyes began to burn. I rubbed them and looked again. There was no question. That painting was the exact same painting as in our castle! It hung in the exact same place along the right-hand wall. In fact, it wasn't just the painting that was identical. I could have been looking into our own library. The entire room was identical, down to the books on the table and the pattern of the rug. Although it was impossible, seeing as this castle was much older than ours, the objects in the room were brighter — the colors in the painting were not as faded as ours, and the rug had retained much more of its color. If ours hadn't been dulled by the sunlight, Mother surely would have tossed it.

I let myself sink down to the grass and leaned my back against the castle wall for support. I thought I might faint dead away. I knew there was a mystery to be found, but I had never expected anything like this!

I spent the night in one of my forts, tossing and turning on the bed of feathers and leaves, snacking on the occasional blackberry, pondering what all this could possibly mean. By daybreak I knew I needed to cut my trip short. I needed Jonathan's knowledge of the world to help me find some answers. I lay my hand on the wall of the old castle and felt a pulse of energy run through my arm. I yanked it away, then felt foolish for doing so. I lay my hand back on the vine-covered wall but felt nothing.

Leaving my potato sacks behind, I took off in the direction of home. In my haste, I tripped over what I thought was a bush. My knee banged against something hard. Bushes weren't supposed to be hard. I turned around to examine it, my hand beginning to shake as I recognized, nearly hidden beneath a tight layer of leaves and branches, the unmistakable shape of a mermaid fountain. And unless I was going crazy — which at this point I certainly considered a possibility — there was water in the bottom of it.

I reached the castle as my parents were finishing breakfast.

"Back so soon?" Mother asked. It was the fourth Friday of the month, so she was in a good mood from whatever she had done the night before. It was unusual for me to be gone such a short period these days, but I couldn't very well explain.

I made some sort of noncommittal grunt, pulled out my chair, and shoved some boiled goose eggs into my mouth. "Do you know where Jonathan is?" I asked between bites.

A quick look flitted between the two of them, and I could see the sympathy in their faces. I sat up in alarm. Had something happened? Had Mother scared him off? Or worse?

"Do not worry," Father said, clearly sensing my fear. "Jonathan is fine. He wanted to tell you himself, but he only had time to pack up his things before the coach came for him."

"He's been promoted to squire and transferred to another kingdom to train for the knighthood," Mother explained. "He was sad to leave here, but this is a very good opportunity for him."

I was stunned. I knew I should be happy for him, but all I felt was abandoned. I slowly rose from my chair; the eggs in my belly felt like rocks. In a daze, I made my way up to my bedroom suite and closed the door firmly behind me.

A note on my dressing table caught my eye. I recognized Jonathan's handwriting and hurried to open it.

"Prince, I am sorry I had not the time to find you in the woods. Everything has happened so quickly. I hope we shall keep in touch, although I know not where this journey will take me. One day when I am a knight, I hope you shall be my king. Your friend, Jonathan."

I lay the letter down on the dresser. My teacher, my guide, my protector, my only friend. All gone in one moment. Now more than ever, I needed to find out the story of the old castle. I needed something to take me away from here. The old castle was the only future left to me.

CHAPTER ELEVEN

ᕫ Princess Rose ᕬ

As much as my bad/terrible/awful painting pleased me, it did not have the same effect on my mother. For months after the painting incident, I often caught Mama looking worriedly in my direction. Since in my family unpleasant things were never really discussed, it took me a while to get up the strength to confront her. Finally, after she had spent almost an entire meal looking at me as if I were a little child whose pet kitten had run away, I had to say something.

When we were alone in the library after supper, I asked, "Mama, why do you appear so sad whenever you look at me? Have I disappointed you terribly?"

Much to my surprise and horror, she burst into tears! I rushed into her arms to comfort her. She stroked my hair and said, sniffling, "Oh, baby, no, don't ever think that. I had always believed the fairies' gifts would protect you and make life easier for you. It helped to soften the terrible blow of the curse hanging over your head. But when you painted that picture, it pained me that you should feel any disappointment or sadness or pain in life. I wanted you always to believe you were the most special, talented, wonderful girl in the world."

"But why?" I asked. "Why do I need to feel that way? Wouldn't you rather I find out who I really am, without the gifts to guide me all the time?"

She sighed. "Honestly? No. I don't want to think of you struggling with anything. I'm not saying it's rational. This is a mother's love talking."

We sat in the two comfortable chairs, holding hands. There wasn't much left to be said. I could not blame her for how she felt. I wondered if someday I would have a child to love as much as Mama loved me.

Later, when she kissed me goodnight in front of my bedroom door, I called down the hall after her. "Mama, for my birthday next week I thought I would cook supper for the family." I hurried through the door before she had a chance to answer. In the morning when I awoke, Sara handed me a note on Mama's personal stationery. It said, *No knives!*

Cook was not as pleased as I thought she would be about my offer to relieve her of her kitchen duties on my birthday night. She argued that she always made something special for my birthday. Was I sure I wanted to mess with tradition? I told her now that I was almost grown up — I was turning fourteen, after all, the age some other princesses were engaged — I really did not need a fuss to be made on my birthday anymore. I had spent the last week working out the menu, and I handed her a list. She read it, grimaced slightly, and nodded.

The morning of my birthday I was up before dawn. I dressed myself since Sara was still sleeping. But instead of my usual gown, I put on an old pair of Papa's nightclothes that he had given me for playing in the garden when I was younger. At first Mama had been horrified that I wanted to wear pants to swing on the swing that hung from an old tree next to the mermaid fountain, but I convinced her I was much less likely to fall without my skirts getting tangled up in the chains. "Safety before fashion," I pointed out. How could she argue with that?

Papa's old nightclothes also made an excellent cooking outfit. I planned on getting dirty today. Sara came in the room, rubbing her eyes and yawning. "Why are you awake so early? The rooster has not even crowed yet."

"Did I not tell you? I am the castle's new cook!"

"Sorry?" she said. "I must have wax in my ears."

I laughed. "I'm cooking our supper today. For my birthday."

"Why?"

"Because I've never done it before. I want to see if I can."

"Like painting a picture?" she asked, taking my hairbrush off my vanity table and directing me to sit down.

"Yes, painting a picture."

As she brushed my hair until it shone, she said, "You know, your painting was not that bad."

"It was supposed to be the garden below my window," I replied.

"Oh." Then after a pause she added, "Well, I'm sure you shall be a better cook than an artist, then."

I wasn't. After a full day of plucking hen feathers, marinating turnips, and churning butter, I hadn't managed to make a single thing that my family could eat more than one bite of. Oh, they tried, to be sure. Papa even had two full bites of the turnip stew before pretending to cough into his napkin. He tried to secretly pass the napkin behind him to a wine steward, but I saw him.

"These plum cakes are delicious," Sara said gamely. She had been chewing the same bite for five minutes. Then suddenly her expression changed to one of great surprise and delight. She swallowed, eagerly reached for her cake, and took another bite.

"You don't have to do that just to make me feel better,"

I said. "I think I let them bake too long. I know they are hor-rid." It would have been nice to make a tasty meal, but after all, very few people did something perfectly the first time they tried it. I had worked hard at doing it and had enjoyed trying something on my own. That was enough for me.

Sara swallowed her second bite and shook her head. "No, honestly, this is delicious. You all have to try it."

My parents had already nibbled on their cakes and were highly skeptical of Sara's claim. The three of us looked at one another and shrugged. We took another nibble. And then another. Before I knew it, we had all polished off our plum cakes and were reaching toward the platter for more. How was this possible? It was like magic. Then it hit me: It wasn't *like* magic, it *was* magic!

I stood up and turned from the table. "All right, Fairy, show yourself!"

At first I saw nothing. Then a foot appeared from behind the purple curtains. It was followed by a leg, and then the rest of the fairy. It was the same fairy who had blessed me with the gift of dance. Everyone else hurried out of their seats. We all gathered around her. I noticed Papa had grabbed another cake before leaving the table and was munching on it behind his large hand.

"What a lovely surprise," Mama said, with a deep curtsy. "To what do we owe this honor?"

The fairy put her hands on her tiny hips. "I could not let Princess Rose create something that was not worthy of her gifts. I had to set things right."

"I do not wish to be disrespectful," I said carefully, "but why? Why can't I do something that isn't perfect every now and then?"

The fairy stood at her full height, which was still only about half of my height, and said, "I need not explain myself to you. Fairies' gifts are meant to be used, not ignored."

"Please, Fairy," Mama said hurriedly. "Rose does not ignore her gifts. Is she not beautiful? Is she not graceful? Does she not sing like a nightingale and dance like a leaf in the wind?"

The fairy waved off Mama's comments. "My job here is done. You might want to take your dessert into the library." With that she jumped into the air and flew right out the window. Unfortunately the window was closed since it was a cold evening. She shook herself off, spit on the window-pane, and it disappeared. She left without a backward glance. The wind whipped through the room.

"Take care of that," Papa said to the nearest steward, pointing to the empty window.

"Why did she tell us to have our dessert in the library?" Sara wondered aloud.

Mama sighed. "I suppose we should go find out."

A steward followed us down the long hallway with a tray of cakes and glasses of cider. When we reached the library, at first we saw nothing out of the ordinary. Then Sara suddenly said, "Look!"

We followed where she was pointing. Where a bookshelf used to be, a painting now hung.

"What is it?" I asked.

"Don't you recognize it?" she said. "That's your painting!"

"What? No! It can't be!" The painting was beautiful. It depicted a young girl lying in the grass, reading a book and gazing up at a pale blue sky. She wore a colorful bonnet.

We all rushed to get a closer look. Mama pointed at the details. "Here is the colorful bonnet I thought I saw when I first looked at the painting in your sitting room."

"And I said I saw a girl who looked like you lying in the grass reading!" Sara said excitedly. "Your initials are in the corner. This is definitely your painting!"

"But how is this possible?" Papa said.

"Fairy magic," I grumbled. Standing on a nearby ottoman, I reached for the painting with every intention of pulling it off the wall. I grabbed the bottom corners to lift it off the hook, but it did not move even an inch. I tried from a different angle. Nothing. I might as well have been trying to pull down the solid stone wall itself.

I stepped back down in defeat. "It won't come off," I said miserably. "She must have affixed it there permanently."

Papa tried, too. But he could not make it budge, either. "I'm sorry, honey," he said, patting me on the head and reaching for another plum cake. "But now everyone will believe you made this lovely painting."

"That's the problem," I explained. "I don't want to get credit anymore for things I don't do. I wanted to do something that reflected *me* for a change. And if it didn't come out well, that was fine." I sank down into a chair.

Mama sat next to me and took my hand. "Rose, listen to me carefully. You are not special and wonderful and admired and loved because a bunch of fairies gave you some gifts. You are special and wonderful and admired and loved because you are YOU. A funny, charming, generous, loving girl with a unique spirit all your own. True, you have some advantages others do not. But that is not why you shine. You shine because of who you are inside."

My eyes filled with tears. "Truly?" I whispered.

"Of course," Papa said, patting me on the head again. "Did you not know that?"

I shook my head. "What do you think, Sara?"

Sara smiled mischievously. "The only reason I'm your friend is because of how well you can sing opera. Without that, I don't know. . . ."

~ 75 ~

We all laughed, and I felt better than I had in years. For the first time, I looked forward to finding out what my life would bring me. If I could live my life happily without needing my gifts, perhaps the curse had no hold over me, either.

It would be a few more years before I learned how wrong I was.

CHAPTER TWELVE

⤙ The Prince ⤚

After Jonathan left I spent nearly a month in the forest. He had taught me so well how to take care of myself that I was never without food and fresh water. Just being near the old castle made me feel better. It still wasn't giving anything up, though. Every once in a while I swore I would hear a low humming sound coming from it, but other than that, nothing stirred or changed, ever.

When I was finally ready to return home, the bailiff informed me that Mother and Father had gone to a meeting in the north with other local kings and queens. I had been left in charge. Without a second thought, I told the bailiff to invite the oldest men and women in the kingdom and the neighboring towns to tea in two days' time. Then I alerted Cook to be prepared with tea and desserts, and told the maids to get out their rags. I wanted the place to shine. I enlisted the pages to help me raise all the windows to let the cool breeze refresh the stale air.

On the following day I filled the mermaid fountain

outside with buckets I borrowed from the stable. Though it leaked in a few places from disuse, the water bubbled happily from the mermaid's mouth.

The falconer saw me from the aviary and came down from his tower. "What will your mother say when she gets back?" he asked.

"I do not care," I replied.

He smiled. "You are planning on getting rid of it before she gets back, right? And you're going to throw some dust back over everything inside?"

"Yes," I admitted. The falconer knew me well.

The next day the bugle blew, announcing the arrival of the townspeople. In all, about twelve men and women showed up. The kitchen staff had set up the tables in the Great Hall, and the room looked nicer than I ever remembered seeing it. The silver serving trays gleamed and the chandelier glittered with light. Most of the guests had never been in the castle before, and I could tell by their twitchiness that they were nervous. Once they were all seated, I stood and said, "Welcome, everyone. Please relax and have some warm tea and cakes." I waited until they were sipping on their tea before adding, "I am hoping you can help answer a question for me."

They whispered amongst themselves at this, then gave me their attention.

I did not want to ask about the old castle directly, so I decided on a roundabout route. "I need to know everything you have heard about my castle," I said. "The history of it, how long it has been here, who built it, anything at all."

This elicited many more whispers, but no one offered up any information. I waited patiently. Finally, one old woman stood up, holding tight to the arm of her chair for support. She was the oldest in attendance, at least eighty.

"My grandmother told me that when she was a girl, the castle was farther away from the town than it is right now. The ground where *this* castle rests used to be a field. Knights and squires practiced jousting here. She said one day, soon after my own mother was born, the castle suddenly moved to this field. Gardens, stables, moat, the whole thing. Just got up and moved all at once! I never believed her tale, of course, for everyone knows castles don't appear fully formed overnight. It must have taken months to move all those stones."

I listened carefully as she spoke and then asked, "How long ago would you say it appeared here?"

She calculated for a moment and then answered, "A few years short of a hundred."

I thanked her heartily, and she sat back down. "Have the rest of you heard the same story?" I asked.

Most of the people in the room nodded. One man stood

up, took off his hat, and said, "I know a bit more, Your Highness."

I nodded my encouragement.

"The castle was moved during the time of King Bertram and Queen Melinda, Lord rest their gentle souls. It was right after their daughter disappeared. They were never the same after that. When they died, the castle went to your father's grandfather, who was from the finest family in the kingdom. Your family has been ruling ever since. Quite well, may I add." He bowed creakily and sat back down.

The story of the daughter rang a bell. My nursemaids used to talk about a missing daughter of Queen Melinda. "Does anyone know more about the girl?" I asked, searching their faces.

One man called out, "I think she was named after some kind of flower. Don't know more than that. I think she was ill or something."

The woman who had spoken first suddenly stood up again. "I remember something else! Grandmother said that when the castle moved, the forest grew triple its size and completely covered the area where the castle had originally rested."

Another woman added, "I've heard those woods are haunted. Ain't natural for woods to grow up that fast." At this, everyone nodded.

Soon they all returned to munching on their cakes and

sipping tea. No one seemed anxious to leave, so I sat with them, mulling over what I had learned. Moving castles? Forests that bloomed overnight? When the last person finally left, I knew what I should have known instantly: King Bertram and Queen Melinda's castle had not moved. An exact duplicate had been created on their fields, and the original was covered by such dense brush and vines as to be virtually invisible. But why? And who had such magic at their disposal as to keep it impenetrable nearly a century later?

I was about to head up to my chambers to ponder further when one of the men came hobbling back inside. "Did you forget something, sir?" I asked.

He shook his head and whispered, "I did not want to say this in front of the others, but I was a friend of your grandfather's, Lord rest his kind soul. When he was a bit older than you, he told me of a vision he had of a beautiful young woman asleep in the woods. He packed a bag and went to find her."

Wide-eyed, I asked, "And did he?"

The old man shrugged. "He wouldn't say. I used to kid him about it, but he would simply smile sadly and say, 'I was not the right one at the right time.'"

"Not the right one at the right time?" I repeated. "What does that mean?"

"I am sure I do not know, Your Highness. I simply

thought you'd like to know the story, since you never knew your grandfather."

"Thank you," I said, reaching out to shake the man's hand. "My grandfather was lucky to have a friend such as you."

"You are a fine young man, Your Highness. He would be proud of you." The man bowed, put his hat back on, and hobbled out.

I could not think of anything I'd done to make anyone especially proud, but I would certainly try to in the future.

That night I dreamt about a girl, except she wasn't a regular girl. For one thing, she had pink wings. For another, she was only about two feet high. In my dream she was handing me a book. I could barely make out the title. *Flora and Fauna of the Northeast Region.* I joked about it sounding very exciting. She did not laugh. I did not remember the dream until I was washing my face in the basin. I stopped in mid-splash and ran it back through my mind. What had the girl-creature been trying to tell me?

I hurriedly finished dressing. Normally Jonathan would be helping me — not that I needed it, of course. I was headed downstairs for breakfast . . . but then I found myself passing the kitchen and heading toward the library. I stood in front of the painting of the girl reading on the lawn. The maids had dusted the painting when they'd been through the castle the day before, and I noticed for the first time how beautiful the girl was, even though the painting was still much more faded and cracked than the one I had glimpsed in the old castle. I tried to make out the artist's name, but some tiny cracks in the paint ran through it. The two initials were either B's or P's or R's, or some combination of them. It didn't truly matter, since I would never have heard of the painter anyway.

But I had not come into the library for the painting. Starting in the far back, I began to carefully search the shelves. I found many books on politics and battles and even a cookbook on how to make the perfect loaf of bread. All the books were covered in a thick sheet of dust, like they hadn't been taken off the shelf in decades. Father was not much into books, and due to my tutors' lackluster performances, I had never been motivated to read much. But now all I wanted to do was find the book from the dream. Three shelves down, I found it. The title ran down the spine, faded, but definitely the same book. I knew it should feel very strange that I dreamt about something and it came true, but at this point I was surprised by little. I pulled it off the shelf, blew off the dust, sneezed, and sat down with the book on my lap. I turned to the first page and held my breath. What secrets would it tell me?

Well, it basically told me all about the flora and fauna of the northeast realm. I already knew what types of trees and vegetation grew here. It was so boring I almost fell asleep. I had to shake myself to stay awake. In the process, I shook something out of the book. I bent down to retrieve it.

It was a thin pamphlet titled "The True and Fascinating Story of a Certain Fairy Who Saved the Princess." A drawing on the cover showed the same girl-creature who was in my dream. I eagerly opened it. In flowery handwriting was a single paragraph:

I, the youngest fairy in the realm, am recording what will likely be my greatest deed in a long, long life. Due to my quick thinking, I was able to lessen a cruel curse made by the eldest fairy in the realm who everyone thought was dead. I alone have ensured Princess Rose's safe passage through these ten decades. I can say no more, for I do not want the wrong suitors disturbing her. Blessings be on the head of the right one at the right time.

That last line sounded familiar. My grandfather! That's the same thing he told his friend upon returning from the woods. Everything began to fit together. The new castle was created almost a hundred years ago — ten decades. No one saw Queen Melinda's daughter after that. The name of a flower — Rose. Princess Rose. P.R. The name on the painting! I twisted my head until I could see it again. That must be her lying on the grass. Did her parents order a duplicate castle from the fairy because they needed the old one to hide her? Could she possibly still be alive behind all those vines?

There was only one way to find out. I ran into the cloakroom and threw on my traveling cloak. The season had grown cold, and I planned on staying in the woods until I got inside that castle. Never had I had such a worthy goal, such a grand mission. My body tingled with anticipation. I was about to tell the bailiff that he was in charge again until my return — but then the bugle blew announcing a visitor. Could my parents be home early from their trip?

A young man stepped in and shook the snow off his cloak. A page came up behind him, holding two suitcases. The young man spoke. "How have you been, old friend? Looks like we're going to be spending a lot of time together."

I gaped. "Percival? What are you doing here?"

"Well, I suppose I've had worse greetings," he said with a grin, draping his wet cloak over his page's outstretched arm. "Did not your father tell you? He invited me to stay at the castle until I am eighteen. He said something about you losing a good friend to the knighthood and that you were taking it very hard. Since there is little chance of me becoming a knight, he thought it would benefit both of us if I came to live at the castle. So . . . where's my room?"

CHAPTER THIRTEEN

～ Princess Rose ～

For my fifteenth birthday I decided to perform again. Now that I no longer felt defined by my gifts, I was happy to share them. I joyfully tap-danced my way across the stage and then playfully went from the flute to the piano and back again. I had written this piece of music in such a way that it sounded like the piano and flute were having a conversation. The audience loved it, and since I had written it myself, I felt like I could rightly share in some of the praise. I was taking my last bow when I caught a glimpse of something in the back row. Since everyone was standing, I could not see clearly. As the audience began to mill about, though, I saw her. It was the old fairy! The one who had cursed me fifteen years ago! Even though I was an infant at the time, I knew her face. She held up an hourglass and slowly tipped it over. "Tick, tick, tick," she whispered. Even though she was on the opposite end of the large room, I heard her clearly. Then she vanished. My heart pounded in my chest. I told no one.

Once the guests left, I ran out to the garden and sat on

the old swing. I had grown much too big to swing anymore, but sitting there brought me comfort. I watched the marble mermaid spit her water into the air, over and over again. She would spit that water forever. I, on the other hand, had no secure future. I figured the old fairy's warning could mean only one thing: Time was running out.

CHAPTER FOURTEEN

⊹ The Prince ⊹

I could not believe Father had sprung Percival on me in this way. No doubt he thought he was doing what was best for me. I had to force myself to be a gracious, princely host. I tried to smile, but I am sure it came out more like a grimace. "Bailiff will show you to the finest guest room, Percival. I must run out, and I am not certain when I shall be back. Please make yourself at home."

I turned toward the gate, but he reached out a hand. "Where are you going? May I accompany you?"

I shook my head. "Just an errand for my father," I lied. "Royal matter. Boring. You shall have more fun here." I knew I should warn him about Mother, but since she was to be away for at least another fortnight, I saw no rush. Hopefully by then he'd have heard it from someone else in the castle. I could not bear to be the one to have to tell him.

"You are the Prince," he said, bowing low. "I shall do as I am told."

I was not so certain of that, but I had more important

tasks on my mind. I left him in the foyer and hurried out the gate. Huddling against the storm, I made my way across the Great Lawn and into the woods. The wind was less brutal here, as the trees offered some shelter. I stopped in at both forts only long enough to collect the tools I had stashed there. While I had tried many times before to cut the vines, perhaps I wasn't trying in the right places. Or perhaps now that I knew the importance of getting in there, it would be different.

I decided to start at the library window. Since there was already that tiny peephole, I figured the vines might be weakest there. I hacked and sliced, careful not to break the window in the process. But it was no use. The vines did not loosen even an inch.

"Shall I give it a go?" a voice behind me asked.

CHAPTER FIFTEEN

～ Princess Rose ～

Every morn I awoke and wondered if I would be waking again the following morning, or a hundred years later. After a few months of this, I decided enough was enough. I would live my life to the fullest while I had it. Every day I took a walk with Mama in the gardens. Or if the weather was bad, she would brush my hair and tell me stories of her own childhood. Papa let me sit in on meetings and taught me to play chess. I began to pay more attention to nature. Sometimes I would sit on a blanket and stare at the grass, just to watch it grow. I helped Mama plant new rosebushes, chrysanthemums, and lilacs. I prayed I would still be around to watch them bloom.

I often went with Sara to visit her family. As crowded as that house was, I loved the boisterousness of it. Children were always laughing and getting themselves into trouble. I wondered sometimes if my parents wanted more children but were scared after the old fairy cursed me. More than anything, I dreaded the fact that sticking myself with that spindle would leave them all alone.

One autumn afternoon I came across the list I had written about the tasks I wanted to undertake. I'd completed that painting (even though the fairy ruined it) and I'd made a whole meal by myself (even though the fairy ruined that, too). The last item on the list was horseback riding. Even though I no longer felt I had to prove myself, I was still eager to feel the wind against my cheeks.

I knew Mama would never let me do it if I asked, so I did not ask. One afternoon I told Sara I only needed to run downstairs for a moment, and instead I ran out to the stables. I had pulled some riding britches out of Mama's closet and wore them under my dress. I quickly shed the dress and asked a stable boy to saddle a small horse for me. I saw him hesitate, but I flashed him a wide smile and he hurried to grab a saddle from the shelf. Sometimes being beautiful wasn't such a bad thing.

He helped me up, gave me a few pointers, and then tapped the horse gently on the rump. The horse began to head slowly out of the stable and onto the lawn. Very, very slowly. Honestly, I thought I could walk faster than this horse was moving. So I dug my heels in lightly, and he picked up the pace to a slow trot. This was great! I loved seeing my familiar surroundings from a whole different perspective. The gift of gracefulness came in handy, because I was very at ease as I bounced up and down in rhythm to the horse's movements.

I was about to enter the woods to take the riding path when I heard shouts coming from behind me. Papa was running toward me, waving his arms. Behind him was Mama, with her long skirts hiked up and her face red, followed by Sara in the rear, who scowled at me. They were all yelling at me to get down, it was too dangerous.

"I am fine, truly," I called out to them. But they kept getting closer. The horse was starting to get a bit jumpy and was shifting his weight from leg to leg. I wanted to tell them to stop yelling, but it was too late. The horse had enough and took off. I yanked the reins like the stable boy told me, but the horse did not stop. If anything, he went faster. He veered into the woods and began jumping over fallen logs and between trees. It was all I could do to hold on. Before I could duck, a tree branch was directly in front of me. I hit it with my head and was instantly unseated. The fall to the ground seemed to take forever.

I am sure I fell very gracefully, though.

As I hit, my vision seemed to turn in upon itself. I saw bits and pieces of my life. The last image I saw was of the old fairy, smiling wickedly and pointing to the hourglass.

Then all was dark.

CHAPTER SIXTEEN

← The Prince →

"Why did you follow me?" I was furious. Of all people to discover the castle! I should have thought to hide my tracks in the snow. It must have been easy to follow my exact route.

Percival shrugged. "I had nothing better to do. What are you up to? Seeing who is stronger, you or a bunch of vines?"

I opened my mouth to reply, but shut it again as I realized he couldn't see the building! All he saw was a mess of leaves and vines, the same things I saw when I first got here. "Um, yes, you caught me." I slowly started stepping away from the castle walls and began swinging my ax at the regular bushes. As I had hoped, his eyes followed me. "I am trying to build up my strength," I continued. "These vines are tough, so they afford an excellent challenge."

"Why did you not tell me this back at the castle?" he asked.

"I was embarrassed," I replied readily. "You are so strong and fit. I did not want you to judge me poorly." I could not believe the words coming out of my mouth. It was worth it, though, if it would keep him away from here.

He clasped me on the shoulder. "I see I arrived at your castle not a moment too soon. We shall start an exercise regimen tomorrow morn. We'll have you fit as a fiddle in no time. Now shall we get back? It is bitter cold."

I desperately wanted to stay, but I could see no way without making him more suspicious. I left the tools where they were and reluctantly followed him back to the house. I planned to return the next day.

It was a full WEEK before Percival let me out of his sight long enough for me to run into the woods. I had begun to suspect that Father may have included watching me as a condition for his stay. Even though Father had not admonished me in years, I knew he did not like it when I disappeared for days or weeks at a time. After all, I was the heir to the kingdom.

The snow had stopped, and I had hoped the warmer weather might have loosened the vines' hold. But no. If anything, the vines were tighter. I pounded against the castle walls, calling out Rose's name. If she were trapped in there, perhaps she could find a way out if I could not find a way in. No response. I called again. "Rose, if you can hear me, go down to the library. Roooose!"

Nothing. Then, from behind me I heard, "Who's Rose?"

Percival was fortunate I had already laid down my ax.

CHAPTER SEVENTEEN

⁓ Princess Rose ⌁

When my eyes fluttered open, it was light. Water soaked my face and hair. I was lying on my bed, with four panicked faces staring down at me. The fourth belonged to the castle physician, who was holding a now-empty bucket of water over my head. I looked up, wiped the water from my eyes, and asked, "Is it a hundred years later?"

"It is an HOUR later!" Sara replied. "And none of us are speaking to you. You gave us a terrible fright. Your poor mother here had to be given smelling salts when we found you lying in a heap upon the forest floor!"

"Forgive me," I whispered, my eyes filling with tears. Mostly the tears were out of guilt from worrying everyone, but they were also because my head ached fiercely and my throat was very dry.

"Is she going to be all right, Doctor?" Papa asked.

The doctor nodded. "Sleep, fluids, perhaps a leech or two. She shall be as good as new. Right as rain."

Mama tossed me a towel, drew my curtains closed, and

went into the sitting room. "You sleep, I shall be right in here in case you need me." Without waiting for my response, she turned and sat down on one of the red velvet couches. Clearly she was still angry with me. I wondered how old I would have to be before I could make my own choices and take my own risks. I was going to be sixteen soon, for goodness' sake. One glance at Mama gave me my answer — I would *never* be old enough!

The castle physician kept me in bed for a full week, which I believed to be excessive. He tried to attach a leech to my leg, but it refused to stick. This may have had something to do with the beeswax ointment I rubbed on before each visit.

Every night I dreamt of horses and how free I had felt. I never dreamt of the fall.

By the end of the week, being laid up in my bed had begun to feel like a punishment. All my meals had been served to me, and stories had been read well into the night, but I missed my walks in the garden and the busy castle life. When I was finally allowed out of bed, the first thing I did was to go downstairs and visit the horse. I wanted to make sure he was all right. The stable boy jumped when he saw me and said, "I'm sorry, Princess, but the queen has given me strict orders not to let you in here."

Why was I not surprised?

He assured me the horse was fine. I tried to sneak a look, but he stepped to the side and blocked me.

I considered sulking for a few days, but that got tiring after only a day. Before the fall, I had truly enjoyed living every moment to the fullest, and I intended to keep that up. For the next few months I kept painting. My horses looked like ladybugs and my ladybugs looked like trees, but I was having fun. My plum cakes slowly improved to the point where we could almost fully enjoy them without the help of fairy magic. I read most of the books in the library, even the boring ones.

For my sixteenth birthday, my parents said I could choose something special to do. I was tempted to ask if I could ride a horse through the countryside but did not want to anger them. It had been years since we had taken a family trip, so I chose that. We decided to go visit the estate of Papa's second cousins. They had a lake where we could swim, which was something I had not done since I was a child. The only body of water near our castle was the moat, and NO ONE wanted to swim in there, considering it was where one of the dung chutes emptied.

Sara was coming with us, of course. She had never been farther than the outskirts of town and we were both ready for a change of scenery. The ride was long, but we made it fun by singing silly songs and guessing what kind of animal would cross the road in front of our carriage next.

I asked Papa if his relatives minded that he was a king while they were just regular nobility. He said that not everyone wants the responsibility that comes with ruling. I had not considered that before. It took a special person to give up their personal freedom in order to protect and provide for hundreds of others. I reached over and gave Papa's hand a squeeze.

The first thing Sara and I did when we arrived was change into our swimming dresses and jump in the lake. We splashed around like two little kids. My cousins joined us. They really WERE two little kids, so we had fun with them. For lunch we were served a whole platter of local delicacies outside on the veranda. We sipped cold tea and tried a little bit of everything. One of the dishes tasted so bad that Sara whispered, "Are you sure *you* didn't cook this?"

After a game of croquet on the lawn, Sara yawned and suggested we both retire to the room we were sharing for an afternoon nap. I agreed, but when we got there I wasn't the least bit tired. Sara fell asleep instantly. I put on some walking clothes and tiptoed out of the room. I felt slightly guilty for not telling Sara I was going out, but how much harm could I get into? Their whole estate was not much bigger than our Great Lawn!

I decided to explore the grounds. Even though the estate was small, it was quite pretty and well kept. I wandered toward a cottage with a thatched roof and a welcoming aroma. In fact, it smelled so good, I decided to knock on the door and ask for the recipe. It would truly impress my family if I could cook something as delicious-smelling as that.

An old woman answered the door and ushered me inside happily.

"You are here to pick up your dress, right?" she asked.

I shook my head.

"Oh," she said, surprised. "When a young lady knocks on my door it is usually to pick up her dress for the big ball. All the eligible men in the area will be there. And you are of marriageable age, are you not?"

I nodded. By sixteen, many girls were engaged to be married. My old friends Bethany and Tabitha had been engaged for a year already. My parents had never tried to fix me up, though, for which I was grateful.

"Well, never mind all that," the woman said. "What can I do for you today?"

I was about to inquire after the delightful aroma, when I noticed a big wheel on a wooden stand in the center of the room. I walked toward it, never having seen anything like it. "What does this do?" I asked.

She laughed. "Why, it weaves things."

I had never seen a wheel that weaves things. "May I try?"

"Of course. Here, you just lift this and pull that and push this, and that's all there is to it."

So I sat down as she instructed, and lifted and pulled and pushed. Two large pieces of wool crisscrossed each other in a beautiful pattern. I'd finally found something I did well the first time. I repeated the steps.

"You are a natural," the woman said. "You might put me out of business." Smiling, she said, "Here, try this, it will make it go faster."

I wasn't watching what she was handing me because at that moment the door banged open and my parents and Sara stood there, out of breath. I grasped the object in my hand at the moment the three of them yelled, "NOOOOOOOO!!!"

I saw the confusion on the old woman's startled face and looked down at my hand. Even though I had never seen one before, I knew without a doubt that what I now held could only be a spindle. I opened my palm wide to release it, but it was too late. A tiny drop of blood had already begun to form on my thumb. Mama ran over and tried to blot it away with her skirt. It stopped bleeding nearly instantly, since it was just the tiniest of holes.

Mama and I stared frantically into each other's eyes, both wide with fear and panic. She was holding on to hope, but I was not. I already felt a subtle change in the air around me. Everyone started to seem far away, instead of crowded around me. They were screaming my name and weeping but I could only faintly hear them. I tried to tell them not to worry about me, that I would be all right. All I could croak out was "I love you." Then all was black. Again.

CHAPTER EIGHTEEN

↤ The Prince ↦

Ever since Percival had heard me calling out for Rose, he had not left me alone. "I shall find out on my own," he threatened, "so you might as well tell me."

I refused. So Percival took it upon himself to use his many connections in town, and eventually found out almost as much of the story as I had. I knew this because every time he learned something new he was only too quick to share it with me. Half the time when I arrived at the old castle, no matter what the season or weather, he was already there with his own set of tools. He even had a special tool made for him by one of the engineers at the castle. Why hadn't I thought of that? I wished the fleas of a thousand armies would take up residence in his armpits.

I watched as he used his new device to hack away at the vines. To my horror and dismay, they snapped! He turned to me with a huge gloating grin on his face, but in that second, the vines curled back in and reaffixed themselves. We couldn't even see where the breaks had occurred. His smile faded.

I left him there, trying again and again, but getting the same result. It finally sunk in, after nearly two years, that neither Pervical nor I nor anyone else was getting in there until whoever or whatever was protecting the princess decided to let us in. That day's events convinced me that until the ten decades had completely passed it was no use trying. The only problem was: I didn't know when exactly that day would be. My only solace was that I was quite certain that Percival was still unaware of the whole hundred-years aspect of the curse. This gave me the slightest advantage.

Weeks went by without Percival ever going into the woods. He studied with whichever tutor was still there on a given day, or he played polo in the fields, or visited friends in town. I did not much care what he did, as long as he stayed away from the old castle. I tried to convince Father to send him back home, but he pointed out that since Percival had arrived, I hadn't run away once. Therefore, he felt Percival must be a good influence on me. I could not explain that the only reason I hadn't run away was that I needed to keep a constant eye on him.

The night before my sixteenth birthday I could not fall asleep. My parents had begun talking of finding me a wife, and Mother even brought some women home for me to meet. One had a lazy eye and a limp, one was thirty years my senior, and another had such a large nose I could not see her mouth when she spoke. Mother, of course, thought they were perfect.

I crept out of the house and into the garden. I had grown much too big for the swing, but I sat on it anyway, hoping the chains wouldn't pull out of the tree. I stared into the mermaid fountain, remembering the day I had filled it when my parents were away. It had been so pretty and soothing to watch. As I continued to stare into it, I thought I heard a gurgling sound coming from it. I peered closer and could swear that just for a split second I could see the water sloshing around. Was the moonlight pulling a trick on me?

I kept watching, but nothing happened. A cloud passed in front of the moon and I yawned. Before I left the garden I went to check on my hidden rosebush. Since it was nighttime, the roses should have been closed up. But one rose shone bright as day. I touched a petal and dew came off on my hand. At that moment I knew: Tomorrow was a hundred years. The fountain, the rose — that's what they were trying to tell me.

I did not sleep all night.

CHAPTER NINETEEN

~ Princess Rose ~

The blackness that came after being stuck with the spindle was different than when I fell from the horse. I could still sense what was going on around me, but I could not explain how. I could not see or hear or feel the touch of hands, but when people were near me, I was aware of it. When they were not, time passed in a hazy, dreamlike way. I knew my family had taken me home. I knew I was in my bed and that the young fairy was somehow protecting me. I could still sense my parents. I knew they were not anywhere in the castle, but that they were still nearby.

Then one day — I did not know how many years later — I could not feel them at all. I wanted to claw my way out of the foggy darkness to find out why, but I could not.

I sensed new people, new families, but they were hazy and distant.

I slept on.

Once, while enveloped in my deep fog, I was aware of a young man outside the castle walls. I could not hear anything, but I knew he was trying to get inside. No one had come this close to me before. I sensed a kindness and a generosity of spirit. I was not frightened. I also sensed the young fairy's presence. The young man left. Every few years he would pass nearby, but he never tried to get in again.

I slept on.

And on.

And on.

One night I sensed a boy outside the castle walls. He was lonely and scared, but curious. He came back often. For the next few years, his visits gently pierced the darkness. I sensed him growing from a boy to a young man. He grew stronger, yet his loneliness never abated. He had a great capacity for love and beauty. Another young man accompanied him sometimes, but I knew no friendship passed between them. I knew all this only in the vaguest sense, the way one knows characters in a dream.

I slept on.

CHAPTER TWENTY

← The Prince →

The morning of my sixteenth birthday I waited impatiently for the sun to rise. At the first glimmer of pink over the hillside, I got out of bed and carefully picked out my clothes. If I were going to meet a princess today, I wanted to look as prince-like as possible. I put on a white ruffled shirt, a red tunic, and black britches. I affixed a small dagger to my belt, and even took a moment to comb my hair.

I crept to Percival's room and pressed my ear against his door. I breathed a sigh of relief when I heard rhythmic snoring. With a happy wave to the early-morning staff, I walked steadily and purposefully across the lawn. My heart began to beat faster as I stepped into the woods. I was so familiar with them, I could have found the old castle with my eyes closed.

The sun threw shafts of light onto the roof of the castle, and dew still shimmered on every leaf and vine. My heart raced with anticipation.

"I wondered when you'd get here, old friend," Percival said, appearing from around the corner of the building.

The color drained from my face. "But . . . but I just heard you snoring."

He waved his hand. "Nah, that was my page, Henry. Sounds like a blacksmith banging on a sword when he sleeps."

I had to swallow hard to keep from screaming. "What are you doing here, Percival?"

"You don't think you're the only one who knows what day this is, do you?"

I took a deep breath. Was this how it would all end? Percival would awaken the princess? I could not let that happen. "Stand aside, Percival. This is my land, and my destiny."

He laughed. "Go to sleep, old friend." Then I saw his arm rise up and felt it come down hard on my head. My legs gave way, and the ground beneath me swelled. I steadied myself with my hands and used all my concentration to shake off the blow. By the time I was able to stand again, Percival was directly in front of the castle door. Since he, too, had figured out it was an exact replica of our own, he knew where the door was hidden. He raised a hand and grabbed at a bunch of vines. He pulled back, clearly expecting them to snap off in his hands. They did not. He tried to let go of them but found them stuck to his hand. I watched in amazement as the vines began to thicken. Before either of us could blink twice, the vines had fully encased him! He screamed, but vines soon covered his mouth as well.

He fell to the ground and rolled a few feet. Looking up at me with pleading eyes, he tried to wrestle free. As much as I disliked him, I could not let him suffocate. I pulled at the vines, trying to loosen them from around his face and neck. I was able to clear a small hole where his nose was, so he could breathe easily. He snorted as he inhaled big breaths of air. I could dislodge nothing else.

"Sorry, old friend," I said to him. "That is the best I can do."

He glared at me as I stepped over him and up to the door. Just as I had always dreamed, the vines parted for me like they were no more than pieces of string. I pushed the heavy wooden door open, expecting it to squeak horribly from disuse. Instead, it glided open smoothly and nearly soundlessly. It felt incredibly strange to be walking through a place that was so familiar and yet so foreign at the same time. I recognized some of the same furniture and the silver tea set, although everything here was much brighter and cleaner. No dust or grime anywhere. The chandelier glowed brightly. How could the oil have lasted a hundred years? This was powerful magic.

I stood in the center of the Great Hall, wondering which way to go. I swore I heard the same faint humming sound as when I was a child. I had not heard it in years. I turned around and raced up the stairs. I hurried past the room that would have been my parents' room in our castle and headed directly toward my chambers. When I reached the familiar door, I hesitated for only a second before pushing it open.

PART TWO

CHAPTER TWENTY-ONE

∾ Princess Rose ᘒ

I knew he was coming before he knew it himself. I had been feeling different lately. Lighter, less foggy and confused. All my senses began to tingle as he approached. No one had been this close to me since time out of mind. The details of my life were still very hazy and disjointed.

I felt his hair graze my forehead. It was the first thing I had felt since Mama's hands in mine. How long ago was that? I did not know. Then I felt his lips press against mine. It was as though he was breathing life back into me. The blood pulsed again in my veins. I heard a bird chirp outside and it was the most wonderful sound I'd ever heard. My eyes snapped open but my head had not fully cleared. Who was this strange man in my bedroom? He was kind of cute. In fact, he was very cute. *Handsome*, that was the word. And tall. I sat up and demanded he explain himself. Normally I would not have been so abrupt, but the situation was very confusing.

The young man told me he was a prince, and that I had

been asleep for a hundred years. My eyes widened as I listened. The memories came flooding back in a torrent. My gentle father, the king. My loving mother, the queen. The fairy's curse. All the dreams where I wasn't quite awake, yet wasn't quite asleep. And now it was a hundred years later and I had been kissed awake by a handsome prince. Well, it was certainly better than having water thrown on my face.

I stumbled out of bed, and he caught me. His arms were strong. He felt familiar to me, and I was not scared. Then suddenly it was his turn to stumble. He turned white and backed away from me, toward my wardrobe. I tried to reach for him before he fell, but I was still too unsteady and could not get there in time. He fell hard against the wardrobe and slowly slid to the floor. Unsure what else to do, and with some cobwebs still in my head, I made my way into the sitting room and filled a bucket with the water that was still sitting, crisp and clear, in my cistern.

I returned to my bedroom, checked the Prince for a pulse, and dumped the bucket of water over his head. I poured the last few drops into my own mouth.

He sputtered and the color returned to his face. His eyes opened, and I could see relief spread all over his face.

Hands on my hips, I asked, "Who is supposed to be awakening who here?"

CHAPTER TWENTY-TWO

↤ The Prince ↦

I laughed as I wiped the water from my face with my sleeve. How good it felt to laugh! I couldn't remember the last time I'd done so. "So you are not a dream, then?" I asked.

Rose pinched her own arm. "Thankfully, no," she replied. "I've had enough dreams for ten lifetimes. What happened to you? You became somewhat green and simply passed out."

How embarrassing! I was supposed to be gallant and brave and strong, and instead I'd fainted right in front of her. "I, er, was hit on the head recently. It must have done more damage than I thought."

Rose went into the sitting room for a moment and returned with a wet cloth. "Here," she said, gently laying it across my forehead. "Keep this on for a while. It will help. I hit my head recently, too."

I wanted to correct her, but I did not have the heart. I could tell that the full gravity of what had happened had not yet fully sunk in. "How did you hit your head?" I asked.

A wistful look crossed her face. "Riding a horse. I could not control it, and a tree branch did me in. It was my first — and only — time on a horse. I loved it."

This surprised me. "I thought princesses grew up riding. I know you have a large stable at your castle."

"Most princesses do ride. My childhood was not typical. You probably would not understand."

"Trust me, Princess. I would understand better than you could imagine. I —"

She cut me off. "Wait a moment. You just said you knew I had a large stable. How could you know that if my castle has been hidden?"

"How can I explain this? My castle is an exact duplicate of your castle. We have huge stables, so I know you must, too."

She stared at me. "How could your castle be an exact duplicate of ours? Do my parents know about this?"

I did not answer right away. "Perhaps you should rest, and we can talk about all this later? This cannot be easy for you and —"

"Now," she pleaded. "I need to understand."

"Very well. Let us go into the sitting room, and I shall fix you a glass of water." I led the way, deftly opened the cupboard, took out a mug, and filled it with water.

I handed her the cup. She took it, sat down on the couch,

then quickly stood up again. "How do you know where everything is?" she asked, a bit suspiciously.

I sighed. "This is my room, also."

"I'm sorry, what?"

I sat on the opposite end of the couch and faced her. "Let me start from the beginning."

"Please do."

And so I told her a bit about my early childhood, leaving out the ogre part and other unpleasant times, and focusing on the parts that had to do with her. I told her of finding the castle when I was a boy, and being determined to find out its secrets. I told her about the rumors of a ghost and the research I did to find out the truth. I told her how the fairy gave her parents the duplicate castle to live in and how my great-grandfather came to inherit the kingdom when they passed away. I told her how my grandfather had tried to get in to find her when he was a boy, but the fairy had sent him home. At this part in my story she turned white and dropped her mug onto the floor.

"My . . . my parents are dead? Since the days of your great-grandfather? Everyone I know and love is gone?"

I knew she wanted to hear me deny it, but my silence told her everything. "I am truly sorry, Princess." I wanted to do something for her. To make it all better. But I was at a loss for what to say.

She stumbled to her feet. "May I have . . . may I be alone for a bit?"

"Of course," I said. "I will be downstairs. I shall fix you something to eat."

She nodded absently. I did not think she even noticed when I closed the door behind me.

CHAPTER TWENTY-THREE

～ Princess Rose ～

I walked over to the looking glass above the cistern and stared at my reflection. I could see Mama's eyes and Papa's jaw. I did not look a day older than when I had pricked my finger, while they were now bones in the ground. I would never know what they went through when I fell asleep, or how their lives turned out. If I dwelled on that pain for too long, I knew it would consume me. Sara's face floated across my mind and it felt like a punch in the belly. Sara! I could not bear to think of us not growing old together. Did she find love? Did she have babies? Was she happy?

I was completely alone now. Not a single lady-in-waiting to watch out for me. Not a soul in the world to love me, not a soul for me to love. I turned away in despair and saw the mug I had dropped on the floor. Maybe there *was* someone after all.

I hurried into the hall and down the stairs. The whole castle was lit up, but it was so very quiet. Never had I heard it like this, even in the middle of the night. I could see out the windows that it was still daylight. Everything looked exactly as I remembered it. If the Prince had not told me a hundred years had passed, never would I have believed it. I found him in the Great Hall, setting two plates of food on the table. It smelled delicious.

"Are you feeling better?" he asked. His concern came through with every word.

I nodded, for his sake. I knew I would never get over the losses I had suffered. I think he knew this and did not question me further. He just pulled out my seat for me and placed a silk napkin on my lap.

"How did you learn to cook?" I asked. "I do not think my father can make . . . I mean, I do not think my father could have made a loaf of blackbread."

"I have to fend for myself a lot. I had a close friend — my page, Jonathan — who taught me how to cook and store food. I apologize for the cold salmon and rice stew. I would have roasted something, but I did not want to alert anyone by sending smoke up the fireplace."

"It's perfect," I said, already halfway done. Between bites, I asked, "Does Jonathan know about me?"

The Prince shook his head. With a pained expression, he said, "I was going to tell him, because I knew he could help me. But he left unexpectedly and I never got the chance."

I could tell whatever had happened to his friend pained

him greatly, and I knew how that felt. I reached out and put my hand over his. We sat like that for what felt like an hour. Eventually I said, "Shall we walk in the gardens? I would love to visit my flowers."

"I would love that, too," he replied. "Our garden has only one rosebush, and even that is hidden amidst the weeds."

"Didn't you say your castle was an exact replica of mine?"

He nodded. "Mother is not the best at upkeep."

Once again, I could tell he was holding back, but I did not press him. I could not wait to feel the breeze on my face again. The Prince led the way down the corridors and into the library. It was still odd that he knew his way around so well, having never been here. He pushed open the door that led to the garden, and the vines melted away from the door, and the garden appeared before us. I stepped through the door and inhaled deeply. The whole garden was in bloom, perfectly manicured and tended. The Prince looked around carefully for a moment, like he was making sure no one was there.

Apparently satisfied, he ran through the paths like a little boy, sniffing one flower and rubbing the petals of another. "Never have I seen such beauty!" he exclaimed. Then he blushed. "Well, except for you, of course. You outshine even your namesake." With that, he picked a red rose and handed it to me. I recalled my first meeting with a rose's thorn, and my eyes filled with tears when I recalled Mama kissing my finger. I turned away before he noticed, though.

"And here's the swing!" he was saying. "And the fountain! Look at her spit that water, it is so wonderful!"

I couldn't help but laugh at his enthusiasm. "You truly love nature, don't you?"

He nodded. "When I was younger, I would watch the grass grow for hours."

I laughed. "Me, too."

He took my hand. His grip was firm. It felt right. "Tell me more about your childhood," he said. We began to walk through the gardens, with me telling him about the fairies' gifts, and how I was always so protected. I even told him about my failures at painting and cooking. When I told him how I had tried to dislodge the painting in the library from the wall, he laughed and said his mother had tried to do the same thing. I could not believe that painting had hung in the new castle for four more generations. Ugh!

It was nice to relive my childhood by sharing it with him. Every once in a while he would interject with something from his youth, but only rarely. Simply from what he didn't tell me I knew it must not have been an easy childhood.

As we stepped out of the garden, the brush and leaves cleared instantly from the Great Lawn. We began to cross it, when suddenly I bumped right against something. The Prince kept walking, but I could not.

"Is something wrong?" he asked, returning to my side.

"I . . . I do not know." I put my hands up and felt in front of me. It appeared to be an invisible, slippery wall. "Something won't let me pass," I said, panic rising. The Prince felt around but could find nothing.

"That is very odd," he said.

I was relieved he did not doubt my words. He suggested we should find out how far it extended, so we walked the entire perimeter of the castle, the vines and brush clearing ahead of us. The invisible wall extended the whole way around. Apparently it was only for me, since the Prince had no trouble walking anywhere.

"Perhaps the fairy is still protecting you for some reason," he suggested. "I think we should go back inside until we figure it out."

I nodded, grateful for his wisdom and his company. He took my hand, and we made our way back to the garden and into the library. A figure stood up from one of the chairs, and we both jumped back. The bright sunlight was behind us and my eyes took a second to adjust.

"What does a girl have to do to get some food around here?" the achingly familiar voice asked.

I gasped and threw myself across the room and into

Sara's arms. She looked exactly the same as the last time I saw her.

"Er," the Prince said, "I'll go make you something right now." He hurried from the room. I was too busy sobbing for joy to pay much mind.

"Who's the guy?" Sara asked. "And does he have a brother?"

CHAPTER TWENTY-FOUR

⊷ The Prince ⊶

I stood outside the library for a moment, long enough to hear the girl explain that when the fairy put the house to sleep, she requested to sleep along with it, and to wake when Rose did. What a truly wondrous and selfless thing to do! I had been dreading having to leave Rose alone when I went back to my own castle, and now I could breathe easier.

I quickly whipped up the same meal that Rose and I had eaten earlier, and brought it into the library. The two of them were talking about their families and how they couldn't believe they were so long gone. They stopped when they saw me and forced smiles onto their faces. I wanted to tell Rose that it was all right to mourn, but I did not want to tell her how to feel or what to do. From what she shared with me, she'd had enough of that in her childhood.

Her friend was introduced to me as Sara, and when I told her I was the Prince, she asked, "But what is your first name?" I had to explain I did not have one, and how Father had said I could choose one years ago, but I had not felt prepared.

The girls exchanged glances. Rose said, "Do not worry. We shall come up with one for you." She thought for a moment. "Eugene? Raphael? Butavian?"

Sara said, "Rufus? Timothy? Philip?"

"Hmm," Rose said. "None of those feel quite right, do they, Sara?"

Sara shook her head.

"I can see I'm going to have my hands full with you two," I said, throwing up my hands in mock exasperation. "I think we need to move on to something more pressing. Why don't we see if Sara can pass the boundaries?"

Rose sobered up. "That is a good idea, Prince . . . er . . . Zeus?"

She and Sara laughed like that was the funniest thing either had ever heard. I was suddenly glad I'd never had sisters.

We went outside and strode across the lawn. Rose walked two paces ahead of me and Sara, holding her arm out in front of her. She stopped when her hand bumped the wall. Sara took a deep breath and stepped forward. "Ow!" she said, rubbing her nose.

"Well," Rose said with a sigh, "I guess we're stuck here together."

I noticed something odd on the ground and got down on my knees. "Look at this," I said. They bent down and I showed them a ladybug that repeatedly attempted to fly from the grass but kept falling back down. It was hitting the wall, too!

I stood up and brushed off my britches. "It appears that anything that was put to sleep along with Rose cannot leave these boundaries."

"Forever?" Rose asked in horror.

"I am certain it is not forever," Sara said, trying to calm her. I was not so quick to make the same claim.

I heard myself say, "I shall figure it out, I promise."

Rose said, "I know you will," and gave me a hug. No one who wasn't related to me had ever hugged me before. I could get very used to it.

The problem of Percival had not been far from my mind. He was no longer outside, so the vines must have released him. I needed to get back to my own castle to make sure he had not alerted my parents to the existence of this one. Striking a prince on the head is not acceptable behavior. He would have to learn that.

"I have to take care of some things at home," I told them. "Will you be all right here? There is plenty of food in the pantry. Everything looks as fresh as if it had been brought in yesterday."

The girls nodded. Sara said, "I do not know if Rose told you, but she is an excellent cook. We will not go hungry."

Rose playfully punched Sara on the arm.

"I will be back before dark. Perhaps before then you could try to reach the fairy to ask about the wall?"

Rose nodded. "I have never called on one of my fairy godmothers before. They have always just shown up, usually when I don't want them to. But I shall try."

She walked me to the door. There was an awkward moment where she tried to hug me and I tried to kiss her, then I tried to hug *her* and she tried to kiss *me*. But then we got it sorted out.

On the walk home, the colors seemed brighter, the air seemed fresher. The love songs the troubadours were always singing suddenly made sense. With an extra skip in my step, I made my way through the woods. Even though the forest was much smaller now, it still effectively hid one castle from the other. In the winter it would be a different story. The skip quickly went out of my step. I had to figure out what was going on with the barrier right away. If the townsfolk learned of Rose's return to life, she would be besieged with visitors — and if the barrier was still up, she would be trapped. In truth, Rose was in more danger now than before I awoke her.

And on top of that, I had to figure out how to tell my parents about her, and how to tell Rose about my parents. I could hear the conversations now: *"Mother, Father, I have fallen in love and wish to marry Princess Rose, the most beautiful girl in the world."* Then Mother's reply: *"I abhor beauty. She is not allowed in my castle."* I did not see the conversation with Rose being any better. *"Darling, I'd like you to meet my mother. Just be sure not to come near her on the second and fourth Thursdays of the month or she may eat you."* And then Rose would say, *"It was lovely knowing you, Prince. Have a wonderful life. Farewell."*

How was I going to make everything work out in the end?

I had absolutely no idea.

CHAPTER TWENTY-FIVE

✑ Princess Rose ✑

After the Prince left, Sara and I decided to take an inventory of supplies. The fairy who'd protected us while we slept must have thought ahead. We had enough clothes, firewood, kindling, soaps, candles, wicks, oil, parchment, ink, and dried meats to tide us over for years. Not that I wanted to spend years trapped in there, by any means.

The only room I had not entered was my parents' bedchamber. Usually at this time in the evening Mama would be there, flanked by her ladies-in-waiting, planning the next day's activities. I could not bear to see it empty. As we passed the door, Sara did not make a motion to enter, either. We hurried past.

"Are you hungry?" she asked, always looking after my needs.

I was, even though I had eaten only hours before. All that sleep must have given me a big appetite. We raided the pantry and found all sorts of delicacies. The Prince was right — everything was very fresh. Chewing on some cocoa beans made me feel a bit better. We were tempted to stoke the embers in the hearth, but as the Prince had pointed out, we did not want to alert anyone to our presence. We made due with chunks of blackbread, quail eggs with vinegar, and cider. Even though the meal left much to be desired, it took our minds off of our situation. Once the food was in our bellies, however, and Sara had cleaned the dishes, we had to face the facts: We were trapped in the castle with no one in the world to care about us except for the Prince.

"Sara?" I asked tentatively, setting my mug of cider on the table. "Why did you do it?"

"Do what?" she asked innocently.

She knew full well what I was talking about, but I played along. "Why did you choose to stay with me? You could have had a normal life, maybe even married a certain squire named Clive."

"Bah," she said with a flick of her wrist. "Clive was handsome, but there wasn't much going on upstairs. He once asked me how one makes ink. Imagine not knowing something basic like that."

I knew she was trying to make me feel better. No matter what she said, I knew it could not have been an easy decision. "What about your family?"

Sara's face fell for a second, but she quickly composed herself. "The fairy gave me time to say my farewells. They were supportive of my decision, although sad, of course. Amelia had recently become engaged to a young man, so she understood that we all have our own paths in life to follow. Granted, right now that path seems murky."

"It's time we did something about that," I said resolutely, pushing back my chair. "Let us find that fairy and get our freedom back."

"That's the spirit!" Sara said.

"Tell me everything the fairy said and did after I fell asleep."

"Well," Sara said, "first your parents and I brought you back here to the castle and laid you in your bed. Your mother sent messengers to the four corners of the realm to track down the fairy, and she arrived the next day. She declared she was going to put the castle to sleep right along with you. Vines and trees would hide it from view. Your parents wanted to stay with you, but the fairy told them their place was ruling the kingdom. They insisted on —"

I interrupted. "My parents wanted to stay with me?" My breath caught in my throat, and I whispered, "And give up their kingdom?"

Sara nodded. "Of course. They *begged* the fairy — and you know how hard it is for anyone to say no to your mother — but the fairy was firm. She said it was their destiny to rule kindly and justly for many years. Your destiny was different. She told them to take comfort in the fact that you were not dead. You would still have many years of life ahead of you. I think that helped ease their pain a bit, but they insisted on remaining nearby. With a wave of her wand, the fairy made a duplicate castle out in the fields, and your parents and all the staff moved there. That is, of course, the castle the Prince's family now inhabits. I had a chance to visit it before the fairy agreed to allow me to stay by your side. Truly an exact replica in every way, except that you weren't there. The fairy said she'd keep an eye on you over the years, to make sure no one entered before it was time. She did not say anything about coming back."

"That figures," I said, adding a deep sigh. "Fairies are notoriously vague."

"So what should we do?" Sara asked.

"Everything we can to find her," I said, determined to free us from these walls. No matter how comfortable and safe it was there, it was not freedom. I yearned to see the world outside the gates. How had the passage of a hundred years changed my beloved countryside? And the town itself? Was it thriving? Did anyone remember the good works my parents had done so long ago?

Sara followed me into the center of the Great Hall. I stood in the exact spot where the fairies had bestowed their gifts (and the curse) upon me a hundred and sixteen years earlier. We held hands. "Good fairy," I chanted, eyes closed. "Young fairy who was so kind to look out for me, can you hear me now? We need your aid one last time."

We strained to hear even a slight fluttering of fairy wings. Nothing.

"What if you gave a little display of your gifts?" Sara suggested. "Maybe that would bring her."

"Good idea." So this time instead of chanting to the fairy, I sang my request and added a little dance move. I wiggled my hips and spun in perfect circles. I tapped out a tune with the silverware on the table. Sara clapped, but the fairy did not show. Dejected, we sat on the lowest step of the stairs, chins resting on our hands.

"Smoke signals?" she suggested.

I shook my head. "We cannot get a big enough fire going."

I noticed through the large windows that the sun had long ago set. "The Prince will be back soon," I said, feeling a glimmer of hope enter me again. "We can ask him to send out word for us."

"Excellent idea," Sara said. "Why don't we go wash up? I feel like I haven't bathed in a hundred years!"

I laughed and followed her upstairs. Without being able to light a fire to heat the water, it was the coldest bath of my life. But I did feel refreshed. Sara helped me pick out a gown to wear for when the Prince returned — one that was not too flashy, but that complemented my eyes. I had never dressed for a young man before. After that, we went downstairs to the library to wait.

We waited and waited. I could feel my eyelids droop. How was it possible I was tired after sleeping a hundred years?

Sara yawned and curled up in her big chair. I could tell she was straining to keep her eyes open, too. "I am sure he'll be here any minute," she said.

I nodded. And that's the last thing I remembered until the sun awoke me. I got up from my chair and went to the window. The dew shimmered on the tips of the flowers. The sky was still orange over the treetops.

The Prince had not come.

CHAPTER TWENTY-SIX

← The Prince →

When I returned to my own castle, one of the young pages told me Father was waiting to see me in the library. I really wanted to go looking for Percival, but I did not want to ruffle any feathers with Father. When I arrived, he was going over some documents with one of his barons. He waved me over and told the baron they would resume their conversation later. The baron hurried out, head bowed.

"Sit down, son," Father instructed. He snapped his fingers and a page brought me some cold water with a lemon on the side. I was usually only served lemon water when I was ill. I began to get nervous.

"We need to talk," he continued.

"We do?" I asked. "Because I am in quite a hurry. I need to find Percival. Have you seen him?"

Father nodded. "That is what we need to speak of. Percival has left the castle and returned home."

My heart leaped. One less problem to deal with!

"However," Father said, "before he left, he delivered

some very disturbing news to your mother and me." Father paused for a deep breath, and then continued, "Percival told us you have been obsessed with an imaginary castle in the woods, and that you have become very unstable, believing you see things — something about a sleeping beauty and fairies. We are very concerned. I knew your behavior the last few years was odd, but I did not realize the depth of it."

I had to grit my teeth to keep from screaming. Percival had devised the perfect plan to assure he would not be punished for striking me. "Excuse me, Father, I must go find Percival. You must not believe a word he says." I tried to get up from my chair, but two castle guards appeared from nowhere and held me down.

"What's going on?" I said, squirming under their grasp.

Father put up a hand and the men released me. "Your mother and I have decided it is in your own best interest to remain here in the castle for a while. You are obviously not well."

I stared at him in shock. "You are keeping me a prisoner?"

Father looked pained. "Please do not think of it that way. All your comings and goings are very disruptive. The castle physician will help you get to the root of your problems."

I could not believe this. "The root of my problems?" I shouted, unable to help myself. "How about the fact that

I'm in love with a beautiful princess who I cannot marry because my mother might eat her! Is that a big enough problem for you?"

"Don't say that about your mother!" Father exclaimed, clasping his hands together. "She hasn't eaten anyone in years, and you know it."

I felt chagrined. Perhaps I did not give Mother enough credit for fighting her ogre urges as well as she did. "I am sorry, Father."

"Yes, well, let us worry now about this imaginary girl-friend of yours."

I opened my mouth to argue that Rose was hardly imaginary, when I realized it would actually be better if he believed her to be, at least for a while longer. I shook my head. "I am tired, Father. May I be excused? I should like to take a nap."

"Of course, of course," Father said. "We will see you at supper. But first, go see your mother."

She was in her sewing room, surrounded by her latest crop of ladies-in-waiting. Mother may have been the only queen in history to darn her own socks, but she said it relaxed her. And in my case, a relaxed ogre-mother was definitely the best kind.

"There you are, son," Mother said, laying the darning needle across her lap. "I want you to meet Giselle." One of the young women hurried to her feet and bowed low. This took some effort, considering she weighed about four hundred pounds. I smiled as graciously as I could, said, "It's been lovely to meet you." I gave a quick bow, and muttering what I hoped was a good excuse, rushed off to my room. The guards were never farther than ten paces behind.

I shut my door, thankful they seemed content to wait outside. I looked around the room helplessly. I stared at my wardrobe and realized it was the same as Rose's. That gave me some comfort. Then the most horrible realization hit me: How was I going to get back to her while under constant guard?

I hurried down to supper although I was not the least bit hungry. Mother had not arrived yet, but Father greeted me with a warm smile. His smile faded when he saw the traveling cloak in my arms. "Father, please, I must go back to the woods. I have an errand to complete. I promise I shall not be long. I'll be back before —"

Father did not even let me finish. "Absolutely not. You will sit down and have a relaxing dinner with your parents, and we can talk about your need to imagine a fantasy life when you shall inherit a whole kingdom someday."

"But I promise I —"

He held up his hand without looking at me and growled, "Do not speak of this again."

My usually mild-mannered father was clearly not going to budge. I couldn't handle this on my own. Instead of joining him at the table, I ran back upstairs and rummaged through my desk until I found parchment and a quill. It would be dark soon and Rose was expecting me. I needed to get this out fast. I scribbled a letter to Jonathan at his knights' quarters. Even though it was late at night now, one of the couriers agreed to deliver it.

Hurry, Jonathan, I prayed. I paced so hard, the rug in my bedchambers was thinning beneath my boots. I watched the stars come out through the window and wiped beads of sweat from my brow, even though it was a cool night. What must Rose be thinking of my absence? Thank goodness she was not alone. I pulled a high-backed chair to the window and stared into the woods as the hours ticked by. How had I believed Jonathan could possibly reach me before morn? Of course he could not.

I watched the sun come up over the treetops and felt utterly miserable. Some heroic prince I turned out to be.

CHAPTER TWENTY-SEVEN

～ Princess Rose ～

Sara laid her hand on my shoulder as I stared into the garden. "He will come," she said firmly. "I assure you. No man looks at a woman the way he looked at you and does not return."

I sighed. "Perhaps he was a figment of our imagination. The fairy could have given us one last dream to prepare us for awakening."

Sara didn't answer right away. Then she said, "Definitely not. Remember your cooking, ah, limitations? Neither of us could have prepared yesterday's salmon and rice stew!"

I brightened. She was right, of course. He HAD to be real. But then where was he? "Do you think something happened to him? Perhaps the invisible wall is keeping him out."

"It did not do so before," Sara observed. "Come, let us begin our day. I am sure he will show up. He seemed the type to keep his word."

I let her steer me out of the library and into the kitchen. Making our own meals was certainly getting old quickly.

What I truly wanted to do was hide in the corner of the wine cellar like I did when I was younger, closing out the world. But I was nearly a woman now. It was time to outgrow such things. I accepted the piece of peach pie Sara found in the back of the pantry, but I could not enjoy its sweetness.

CHAPTER TWENTY-EIGHT

⊰ The Prince ⊱

By noon the courier had still not returned. Perhaps he had not even located Jonathan. As a knight, he could be off somewhere distant on a quest. I had no way of knowing. A tray of breakfast food had been delivered to my chambers earlier, but all I could choke down was one sausage. The porridge now sat in the corner, congealing.

I stared out onto the lawn. The falconer was there, working with his birds. Every few moments one of them flew dangerously close to my window but turned before smacking into the thick glass. I feared I might go mad if I sat there any longer, so I decided to join the falconer on the lawn. The guards were surprised by my sudden appearance in the hall and scrambled to their feet. I did not give them a backward glance. Fortunately they dared not stride too close to the birds so I was given a wide berth. The birds were used to my presence, but to a stranger they could be deadly.

"What troubles you, Prince?" the falconer asked, not turning around.

"How do you know I am troubled?"

He cocked his head toward the birds, circling a few yards above us. "The birds can always tell. They have sensed your distress. In addition, I do not recall seeing the castle guards posted to your care since you were a babe."

I sighed. "You would not believe it if I told you."

"Try me," he replied, holding out his arm. A falcon landed neatly on the thick leather strap and accepted a small piece of fresh meat before flying off.

Before I could stop myself, the whole story came pouring out. Princess Rose and the invisible barrier, Percival and his lies. The castle guards. When I was finished, the falconer watched the birds circle for another moment, then said, "You shall have to move quickly."

"I know," I replied. "Every hour seems like a year to me."

He shook his head. "It is more than that. Your father has asked me to prepare the birds. He is planning a hunt for tomorrow."

I gasped. "He shall find the castle!"

"You will have to reach Rose before that happens."

"What can we do? I can run swiftly, but I cannot outrun the guards. They would surely pursue me."

"I shall help you," the falconer said. He walked a few paces farther from the castle, keeping his eyes focused on the air so the guards would think he was just following the patterns of the birds. I followed. "The way I see it," he said softly, "you must get word to the princess of your situation. I can send my swiftest peregrine with a note. Then tonight, under the cover of darkness, I shall cause a distraction — perhaps I visit the aviary and some falcons are missing. Your father will call for an immediate investigation, and your guards, believing you to be sleeping in your bed, shall be called to help. You will then flee into the woods and return to your princess. Even if you have not figured out how to grant her total freedom, at least you will be together when the hunting party arrives at her door."

"I do not know how to thank you," I said humbly.

For the first time, the falconer met my eyes. "I have known you since you were a babe and watched you grow. Your life has not been easy. You deserve your happiness now. I shall prepare the note, telling the princess you will be there before midnight."

I grasped him on the shoulder in thanks. For the rest of the day I was a dutiful son. I helped Mother organize a charity dinner. I sat in with Father as he met with the bailiff about something to do with taxes, a sick goat, and a barrel of ale. I couldn't focus enough on their conversation to figure out what those three things had to do with one another. I was too busy planning my escape.

At supper, Father spoke of his plans for the hunt. Mother said she'd like to come along and Father said that would be fine. I began choking on my pheasant. The steward brought me some water. I gulped it down as I quickly calculated the date. We were still four days away from the second Thursday of the month. We were just about to begin the apple cobbler when the porter came in and cleared his throat.

"Excuse me, Your Highnesses, but the Prince has a visitor."

I jumped up from my chair. Could Rose have broken through the barrier? If so, I needed to hide her from Mother! Or maybe the visitor was Jonathan!

"Show him in," Father said, obviously pleased with the thought I might have a friend.

The porter shook his head. "The visitor told me he should like to see the Prince in private. He says it is a matter of state business."

Father looked confused.

The porter continued, "Something about the work the Prince is doing in the village, in Rose Square? Helping the townspeople?"

My heart thumped in my chest. Rose Square! Whoever this visitor was, he or she knew something about Rose! "Oh, yes," I said hurriedly. "I know what this is about. I've been helping to plant some new rutabagas and turnips in Rose Square. I shan't be long."

Mother wore a pleased little smile. "You go on, son. What a lovely way to help the less fortunate."

I nodded and followed the porter from the room. Mother gestured for the guards to stay behind, which was kind. The porter led me to the library. A very short man in a black cape was facing away from me. He waited until the porter left us to turn around and lift his head. I almost fell over backward, quickly steadying myself on the arm of a chair, amazed by the disguise.

"You must be . . . you're . . ." I stuttered, not being able to form the right words.

The creature nodded and curtsied slightly. "I am the fairy who has looked after Princess Rose for lo these many years. I looked after you, too, although you did not realize it."

When I could catch my breath I said, "You did an excellent job of keeping Rose safe, and I thank you deeply for allowing me to be the one to awaken her. But why can she not leave the grounds of her castle?"

"Oh, but she can," the fairy said with a shrug. "Just as soon as you let her."

I almost fell backward again. "Me? Whatever do you mean? What could it possibly have to do with me?"

The fairy sighed, shaking her head. "Men. Do you understand nothing? I shall tell you this much:

Until both worlds unite
in welcome harmony,
past and present as one
shall not grow to be."

And with those cryptic words, her features began to shimmer and I had to squint to see her. Then she was gone. Just gone. Cape and all. I stared at the space she had previously occupied.

"Fairy!" I whispered loudly. "Please come back. What does that mean?"

I caught a faint shimmer near Rose's painting on the wall, but it quickly disappeared. The fairy was not coming back. Thankfully I would see Rose soon. I hoped she had better luck with the fairy than I.

CHAPTER TWENTY-NINE

~ Princess Rose ~

"What is *that*?" Sara asked, pointing above our heads. I laid down my paintbrush and looked up from my easel. It had been Sara's idea to take out my old art supplies, and we had spent a peaceful hour in the garden, painting. The missing prince was never far from my mind, though. I had to put up my hand to shield my eyes from the sun. A dark shadow passed back and forth, circling overhead. It gradually got lower until I could clearly see it was a large falcon. I had not thought to check the aviary when Sara and I toured the castle yesterday. Had some of the birds possibly survived? But no, this one did not have our family's colors on its talon.

"Should we go inside?" Sara suggested, backing away. "Those birds can be very dangerous."

I shook my head. The bird was gliding to a halt on top of one of Mama's prized blueberry bushes. It shook its leg. "I think it's hurt," I said, stepping toward it.

"Careful," Sara warned, coming up from behind. We

slowly approached the bird, trying not to make any sudden moves. About two feet away, I realized the bird had not hurt its leg — it had a note tied around it! It was holding out its leg so I could take it. The bird bent its neck down to sample a blueberry and I took that moment to slip the scroll out from under the thin leather band that bound it. I unraveled the thin parchment. "It is about the Prince!" I exclaimed.

"Out loud, please," Sara demanded.

"'Princess Rose and Lady Sara, the Prince is under house watch and could not come as promised last night. He feels terrible about it, and shall rectify the situation tonight. Please look for him before the midnight hour. Blessings, the falconer, friend of the Prince.'"

I read it over and over until Sara finally cleared her throat. I looked up, blushing.

"Shall we send a reply?" she asked. "The bird is still here."

"Excellent idea." I hurried over to the easel and picked out my thinnest brush. I turned to my palette and dipped the brush into some blue pigment. With my hand poised over the back of the scroll, I suddenly stopped. I had never written a note to a young man before. What was I to say? The bird flapped its wings impatiently.

I wrote: *I shall count the hours. Yours truly, Princess Rose.* Then I gently waved the paper in the air for a few moments so it would dry before I rolled it back up. I affixed it to the waiting leg, and as soon as I tightened the leather knot, the bird flew straight up and away.

"What was your reply?" Sara asked.

I told her and she looked aghast. "*Yours truly?*" she said. "That sounds so formal!"

I lifted my chin defiantly. "That is how Mama used to sign her letters."

"Yes," Sara said, "when she was writing to a friend, or ordering more clothes. Not when she was writing to her one true love."

I pretended to be absorbed in my painting. I couldn't very well sign it *With love, Rose.* After all, I had known him for a day. True, my heart did quicken whenever I thought of him. And I had felt comfortable with him very quickly. But I had never known love for a young man before. How was I to recognize it now? Without taking my eyes off the flower I was painting, I said, "In my defense, I DID say I was counting the hours until his visit. Surely that was bold enough?"

"True," Sara acknowledged. "That was in the right spirit. Fine, I shan't mention *yours truly* again."

"Yes, you will."

Sara shrugged and smiled in that mischievous way of hers. "You are probably right."

That night as darkness fell, Sara and I went into the

library to wait. We huddled together on the couch under the warmest blanket we could find, still not daring to light a big fire. I tried to keep myself awake by recalling the Prince's features one by one. His long, regal nose. His warm brown eyes. His hair the color of sunflower oil. I was just about to dwell on his broad shoulders when Sara grabbed my arm and we both sat bolt upright. Shouting! Someone was shouting outside. More than one someone. My heart pounded in my chest. One voice cried out above the others, "Open the door! Open the door!"

I could not move.

CHAPTER THIRTY

← The Prince →

I watched out my window as one star after another filled the night sky. When I was younger I used to believe that the night sky was a black curtain with pinholes stuck in it that let the tiny rays of sunshine through. But Jonathan had studied astronomy and said that I was wrong, although he could not tell me what the tiny lights were. Tonight I knew exactly what they meant — that I would be seeing Rose soon.

I blew out my oil lamps and climbed into bed noisily, so the guards posted outside my door would be sure to hear. Under my nightclothes I was fully dressed. After what seemed like hours, I finally heard the bell gonging in the tower, indicating someone had cause for alarm. The guards began arguing. I could not make out their words through the thick wooden door, but I assumed they were deciding whether to go or not. I quickly began snoring as loudly as I could, tossing in a moan every now and then, like I was having a nightmare. This must have convinced them, because moments later I heard their boots stomping away down the hall.

I counted to ten, tossed my blanket off, and ran out the door. I kept to the shadows, creeping along the hall and down the stairs. I dared not cross the Great Hall, because I knew Father would gather his men there. Instead, I crossed the foyer and exited through the door the dung cleaner uses to clear the privy. I held my nose until I was through the small tunnel and out into the night.

Filling my lungs with the crisp, fresh air, I took off at a run, not looking behind me. Had I done so, I would have seen the group making its way to the aviary and I would have waited another minute. As it was, a shout rang out. I had been spotted! I still had the advantage. They did not know the woods and would have to stick to the paths. I did not know if they thought I was the falcon thief or simply myself, the escaped Prince, but that did not matter. They were in hot pursuit.

I hopped over fallen logs and ducked under tree branches, grateful that the leaves were not crunchy underfoot. I could still hear the guards shouting and calling out behind me, although they had fallen farther back. I forged ahead through the woods and broke into a straight run once I hit the lawn. By the time I reached the gardens, I knew there was not a second to waste. I saw a faint light in the library and called out for Rose to open the door. She must not have heard me. I had almost reached the castle when I saw her face through the window . . . and then it disappeared.

A second later, the door flew open.

CHAPTER THIRTY-ONE

~ Princess Rose ~

The Prince bolted the door behind him and leaned against it, breathless. "Are you two all right?" he asked between gasps.

I nodded. "I would ask the same of you. What is happening?"

"It's a long story," he said. "We need to hide first. But where?"

I knew just the place. "Come with me," I said, grabbing the blanket from the couch. The Prince grabbed one oil lamp, and Sara the other. I led the two of them down the cold stairs to the wine cellar.

"Ah," said Sara, "your old hiding place."

"You knew about it?"

She nodded. "Everyone knew about it."

Of course they did.

"I've only been down here a handful of times," the Prince mused from behind me. "I mean, down to our own wine cellar, of course."

"Why so infrequently?" I asked, winding through the racks of wine and barrels of ale.

"My family does not do much entertaining. We have little need of a full larder such as this."

From the rear, Sara said, "But I thought all kings and queens entertained. Rose's mother loved to."

"Queen Melinda," the Prince said.

I stopped short, and they almost bumped into me. "You know of my mother?"

He nodded. "Queen Melinda was our kingdom's most beloved queen. My mother is well-liked, too, but everyone has heard of the generosity and goodness of Queen Melinda."

Tears pricked at the back of my eyes and my heart filled with pride. We kept walking. "So why do your parents not entertain?" I asked, forcing myself to remember that this was my life now, here, in the present.

"Mother is not, ah, shall we say, always great with new people."

"Is she shy?" I asked.

"No," he said after a pause. "Not shy, exactly."

I would have pressed further, but we had reached my nook.

"This is perfect," the Prince said when he saw it. "Even

if the castle guards get in the house, they would never spot us down here."

We crawled into the nook and spread the blanket around us. It was actually quite cozy. The Prince took my hand and my heart started racing. "Now, Prince," I said, hoping he could not hear the quiver in my voice, "do tell us who is chasing you and what kept you last night."

So he told us about his parents putting the guards on him, and the falconer's plan, and about being chased here. And then he got to the part about the fairy and her cryptic message.

"Fairies!" Sara exclaimed. "Why do they have to be so mysterious?"

"At least you had better luck than we did," I told the Prince. "The fairy would not even come to us."

"I cannot take any credit. She came unbidden, although I was very glad to see her. I was hoping you would know what she meant."

I repeated her words to be sure I had them correct.

"'Until both worlds unite
in welcome harmony,
past and present as one
shall not grow to be.'"

The Prince nodded.

"That is a pretty sorry rhyme, if you ask me," Sara muttered.

"Both worlds unite," I repeated. "Both worlds unite. Papa always told me to consider the simplest option first. So in this case, both worlds probably mean your world and mine, past and present." I smiled, pleased with my deductive reasoning. The fairies didn't give me that gift of intelligence for nothing.

The Prince nodded and said, "But our two worlds *did* unite. We're united now."

My smile faltered. He was right, of course. We fell silent and thought hard on what else the words could mean.

A loud noise interrupted our contemplation. We all stiffened. I tightened my grip on the Prince's hand. He whispered, "Do not worry. I bolted the door. They cannot get down here without a battering ram, and I doubt it will come to that."

I nodded, still clenching his hand. Then it suddenly hit me. What were we afraid of? We had done nothing wrong. I was about to give voice to this, when suddenly the Prince said, "What are we doing? We are hiding from my own guards? We did nothing wrong. We just want to be together!"

"I agree!" I said, feeling a rush of affection for him.

"Hey!" I said, jumping to my feet and almost hitting my head on the shelf above us. "I know what the fairy meant!"

The others got to their feet, too. "Do tell," they said.

"Our families are a part of who we are, right?"

They nodded, the Prince a little hesitantly.

I continued, "So our worlds have not united until your parents have welcomed me with harmony! Then my past and your present shall be one, and I shall be free to join you in your castle!"

The Prince's face drained of its color.

Oh, no! I had obviously spoken too freely. "Um, unless you do not want me to join you in your castle?"

"Er, I'm just going to check out that ale barrel on the other side of the room," Sara said, quickly scuttling away.

"No, no," the Prince said, taking my hands in his. "I want that more than anything. It is just that . . . that . . ."

"What is it?" I asked, relieved I had not overstepped. "You can tell me anything."

He shook his head miserably. "I do not know if I can tell you this. You might not want to be with me, and I could not bear that."

I wanted to tell him he was being as cryptic as the fairy!

The voices overhead suddenly became louder. "Son, we know you are down there."

"It's my father!" the Prince whispered.

"Son, please let us in. Your mother and I are very worried. What is this place? How could it possibly be what it looks like? Please, we need to talk."

"He sounds quite reasonable," I whispered.

"He is," the Prince said. "It's my mother I am worried about."

"You may not have noticed this," I said, smoothing down my skirts, "but I can be quite charming. I am sure your mother will like me, and I her."

The knocking was getting more forceful.

"You do not understand," the Prince said, clearly anguished. "My mother will not let you in our castle."

I put my hands on my hips. "Why on earth not?"

He sank to his knees. "Because you are so beautiful."

Well, that was nice to hear. But it did not make the least bit of sense. "Sorry?" I said. "What was that again?"

He would not meet my eyes. "My mother has banned all things of beauty from the castle. She has a bit of ogre blood in her and cannot stand to be around beautiful objects or people."

Now *that* I was not expecting to hear. "Your mother is an . . . an ogre?"

"Only slightly," the Prince said miserably. "Most of the time she is a normal, if slightly odd, woman. But on the second and fourth Thursdays of every month, her ogre blood surges and she . . . she . . ." He buried his head in his hands and I had to kneel next to him to hear the words. "She has to feed."

"Feed?" I repeated. "Feed on what?"

"Anything that is close at hand," he said. "Goats, cows. People. I wanted to keep you from all this. I have lived with it my whole life, but you should not have to. I will understand if you never want to see me again."

I put my hands under his chin and lifted his head. "You and I are in this together," I said firmly. "We will figure out a way to make this work."

The corners of his lips lifted. He lightly traced the side of my face with his finger. I knew at that second that I truly did love him. He leaned in and kissed me. Our third kiss. (True, I was half-asleep for the first one, but I still count it.)

"If only you were not so fantastically beautiful," he whispered in my ear.

"Oh, that is easy," I said. "Watch." I bent down and ran my hands along the soot and dust on the cold stone floor. Then I wiped the dirt all over my face. I leaned over and took a pair of shears that hung on the wall and haphazardly chopped at my hair until it was all different lengths. When I was done, he was gaping at me, his jaw practically hitting his chest.

"I cannot believe you just did that for me."

"I did it for *us*," I told him. No need to add that by tomorrow I would be beautiful again, hair fully restored, thanks to the fairy's "blessing." I would just have to keep up the routine daily.

He took my hand firmly and we headed toward the stairs. The knocking had stopped, but we knew they were still up there. When Sara saw us heading toward her, she stopped pretending to examine the ale barrel and joined us. When the light from her lamp hit me, she stopped short. "I leave you for ten minutes and this is what happens?" she exclaims. "Have you gone *mad*?!"

I laughed. "I am not mad! Do not worry. There is no time for a real explanation. I have to pretend to be ugly so the Prince's mother will like me."

"What?" she asked, looking back and forth between me and the Prince.

"I shall explain later," I promised as we climbed the dank stairs. "But you might want to smear a little dirt on your own cheeks, just in case."

"This better be good," Sara muttered, sweeping some dust from the wall with her fingertips. "Or you are in *big* trouble."

CHAPTER THIRTY-TWO

⤙ The Prince ⤚

I unbolted the door and together we stepped into the hallway, blinking against the glowing dawn. Before us stood my parents, a mixture of concern and bewilderment on their faces. They did not look angry, though, and I could see none of the guards. Mother was leaning against the wall, fanning her pale face with her hand. All the bright colors in this castle must have been overwhelming to her.

"You must be the Prince's parents," Rose said, curtsying to them both in turn. "I am Princess Rose. Perhaps you have heard of me?"

They both shook their heads but peered at her with curiosity. I kept my grip on Rose's hand and said, "Princess Rose is the daughter of King Bertram and Queen Melinda."

"But they lived a hundred years ago!" Mother exclaimed. "I seem to recall they had a daughter, but she disappeared."

I nodded. "This is she. Rose was put under a curse and was asleep for a hundred years, hidden right here in this castle. Right on our own property."

"Astonishing," Father said.

"The prophecy said the right person would awaken me," Rose explained. "The Prince, your son, was that person."

"And this castle?" Father said. "It is identical to ours in every way!"

"The fairy's magic," I said. "When Rose fell asleep, the whole castle went to sleep with her. The fairy duplicated the castle and Rose's parents lived out the rest of their reign there. Then Great-grandfather took over the kingdom, and our family has lived there ever since."

"I am sorry I doubted your word," Father said, clasping me on the shoulder. "I had heard my grandfather tell tales of a hidden girl, but I thought they were only tales. I shan't doubt you again."

"Thank you, Father. I know you thought you were doing what was best for me."

Mother stepped forward. I watched her take in Rose's ragged hair and her dirty face. She lifted Rose's hand — the one I wasn't gripping — and examined her fingernails. They had dirt under them. A wide smile began to make its way across her face. "Welcome, dear," she said, kissing Rose on both cheeks. Turning to me, she said, "You have chosen well, my son."

I beamed. Father stepped forward and kissed Rose on

the cheek as well. Then he whispered in my ear, "She is the girl in the painting in our library, yes?"

I nodded, glancing at Mother to make sure she wasn't listening.

He winked and echoed Mother's words. "You have chosen well, my son."

I wanted to sweep Rose into my arms, but before we had a chance, the walls seemed to sway a bit. I felt for a brief second the same dizziness that accompanied Percival's blow in the forest. The tapestries billowed out, and we all reached for them to steady ourselves.

"What was that?" I asked, alarmed.

"Look at the tapestries," Father said, the awe evident in his voice. "They have faded. They look like ours now."

It was true! All the bright colors had faded away. At the same moment we all turned our heads to the sounds of voices filling the air around us. The cooks in the kitchen, the squires in the fields, the maids arguing over whose turn it was to sweep out the pantry.

"Um," Rose said, looking around, "I don't think we're in my castle anymore."

"How can this be?" Mother asked, the color returning to her cheeks.

I turned to Rose and grinned. "This means the fairy has

lifted the wall! You are in my home now." The joy I felt having her here filled me to bursting.

Rose tentatively looked around. Expressions of sadness and joy alternately crossed her face. "I have a hunch there is only one castle now. I think we should only find trees in the forest."

As soon as she said the words, I knew they were correct. "I promise to make you feel at home here," I said.

She squeezed my hand tight. "I know you will."

"Ahem," a voice said from the top of the cellar steps. "Remember me?"

ᴗ Princess Rose ᴄ

I laughed. "Forgive us, Sara. Your Highnesses, allow me to introduce my lady-in-waiting and best friend, Sara. She has only recently awoken as well."

Sara had not shorn her hair (thankfully, since it would not regenerate overnight like mine would) but she had smeared her face convincingly enough. She even blackened out a tooth. Fortunately Sara did not ask any questions of the Prince's parents, only throwing me a look of daggers every now and again.

From where I stood, I could see a tall young man in a knight's garb striding toward us. The Prince had his back to the man, but Sara saw him. Her jaw dropped. The man looked enough like our old squire Clive to be his brother.

A deep voice rang out, "Is that my long-lost friend, the Prince? The one who is very poor at correspondence?"

The Prince's face lit up. He whirled around. "Jonathan!" They clasped hands. "I thought I would never see you again."

"I arrived as fast as I could," Jonathan said. He glanced

over at me and raised an eyebrow. "But it looks like you do not need my help any longer."

"Come, my Queen," the Prince's father said, taking his wife by the elbow. "Let us give the young people their privacy."

Once they headed down the hall, Sara stepped behind us and began furiously wiping the dirt off her cheeks.

"Old friend," the Prince said, "allow me to introduce Princess Rose. She has stolen my heart and I hope she never gives it back."

I blushed under my soot as the young knight bowed. "I do not always look like this," I whispered.

But Jonathan was no longer looking at me. He had turned his full attention to Sara, who had stepped out from the shadows. I elbowed her and drew my finger across my teeth. She got the hint and ran her tongue across her teeth to loosen the soot.

The Prince made the introductions. Sara said, "Forgive my staring, but you look exactly like someone I used to know."

"Who would that be, my lady?"

"A squire who served under Princess Rose's father. His name was Clive. Honestly, you could be his double."

"I had a grandfather named Clive," Jonathan said, never taking his eyes from Sara's.

Sara's face fell. She said, "I suppose you don't know how to make ink, either."

"Egg whites, soot, and honey," Jonathan replied without a pause.

Sara's face lit up again. The Prince laughed. "There is not much Jonathan does not know."

"Would you like to go for a stroll in the garden?" Jonathan asked Sara.

Sara nodded. Jonathan held out his arm and Sara linked hers inside it. To me she said, "I trust you won't further destroy your appearance before my return?"

"On my honor," I said. Satisfied, they left without another word.

"Wow," the Prince said as we watched them go.

"I know!" I replied.

He turned to me, his face shining. "We have the whole world to explore. Where would you like to go?"

I thought for a moment. "Wait here, all right? I want to check something."

He nodded, and I hurried down the hall, past the eyes of the unfamiliar staff, and took the tall steps two at a time. Once I got to the top, I ran down the hall toward where my room had been in my own castle. Here there was another door next to mine, where at home there had only been a blank wall. I cautiously pushed open the first door and breathed a sigh of relief. My whole room was here, with all my clothes, and all my memories. I closed the door and moved onto the next one. I pushed it open and peered inside. The room itself was identical to mine, except it was the Prince's for certain. I could see his traveling cloak slung over the chair. I smiled to myself. The fairy had taken care of everything. I hurried back downstairs. The Prince was just coming out from the cellar.

"The oddest thing," he said. "I was suddenly curious to see if the blanket we had used for warmth in the cellar was still there."

"Was it?" I asked, my curiosity piqued.

He shook his head. "It was not. But something else was in its place, hidden by decades of cobwebs." He reached behind him to reveal a small wooden crate with faded red pigment on the top. "Let us go into the library and I shall show it to you."

I followed him in there. It was just like our library, except with fewer objects of art, and the rug on the floor was much less colorful. I was pleased to see my painting that the fairy had "fixed" was quite faded as well. He rested the box on a small table and said, "I believe this is yours."

"Mine? I have never seen it before." I peered at it and wiped the thick dust off the top. A picture of a red rose appeared. I eagerly pushed the top open and looked inside.

There, tied with a red ribbon, lay dozens, no *hundreds*, of letters. My heart literally stopped beating for a moment as I stared. I recognized Mama's hand and Papa's, too. I even recognized the neat printing of Sara's sister, Amelia. I untied the ribbon and let my fingers run through the letters, unable to believe it. They must have written these over the course of their whole lives. I thought I might faint from the joy of it. What an incredible gift they gave me.

"They must have hidden the box in the nook because they knew you used to hide there," the Prince said. "Imagine — they have been in the castle my whole life and I never knew it."

"Thank you for finding them," I said, tears streaming down my cheeks.

He blushed. "You would have found them eventually."

"Perhaps not," I replied. "I have nothing to hide from now."

He brushed some soot away from my cheek and kissed the spot. "I thought you should know," he said softly, "I have finally come up with my name."

"Wonderful," I replied. "Do tell. No wait, is it Boris?"

He shook his head.

"Rupert?"

"Nope."

"Montgomery?"

He got down on one knee and took my hand in both of his. "No, it is not Montgomery or Zorro or Quince or any name you have ever heard. I should like my name to be only one thing — Princess Rose's Husband. What do you think?"

I felt a tingle in my toes. Having my parents' letters with us made it feel like they were giving us their blessings. "Princess Rose's Husband," I repeated, laying my hand on his shoulder and smiling wider than I've ever smiled before. "I think it has a lovely ring to it. And just think, you would be the only man in all the realm to have that name."

"Forever after," he said.

"Forever after," I agreed.

And life was good. Very, very good.

About the Author

Wendy Mass is the author of the award-winning books for young readers, including *A Mango-Shaped Space, Jeremy Fink and the Meaning of Life, Heaven Looks a Lot Like the Mall, Leap Day, Every Soul a Star, The Candymakers*, and the books set in Willow Falls, *11 Birthdays* and *Finally*. She loves writing the Twice Upon a Time series because who's to say it *didn't* happen this way? Wendy lives in New Jersey with her family. You can visit her online at www.wendymass.com.